Andrea

"THE BEGINNING"

HOLY TRINITY BOOK ONE

ADRIANA BRINNE

Andrea (Holy Trinity #1)

ISBN: 9798573424026

Cover Design Cat at TRC Designs
Formatting by Juliana Cabrera, Jersey Girl Design
Editing by Elsa Gomes (bookishaurora)

To my hero.

I love you endlessly, blindly, and madly.

You have loved me in every chapter of my life, through the good and bad and I wouldn't be me without you. I am not an easy child, I gave you hell once or twice, but still, everything I do in life I do it to make you proud.

To my mami, you inspired Valeria.

Just like Andrea is nothing without her mom, I am nothing without you.

Playlist

"Breathe" – Little Mix
"Young God" – Halsey
"Sad Eyes" – James Arthur
"Monster In Me" – Little Mix
"Midnight Sky" – Miley Cyrus
"Sicko Mode" – Travis Scott
"Therefore I Am" – Billie Eilish
"No Peace" – Sam Smith Ft. Yebba
"Highest In The Room" – Travis Scot
"Slow Motion" – Charlotte Lawrence
"Hate Me" – Ellie Goulding
"You Broke Me First" – Tate McRae
"Kiss Me Goodbye" – DeathbyRomy
"Lose You to Love Me" – Selena Gomez
"Off the table" – Ariana Grande Ft. The Weeknd
"Die For Me" – Post Malone Ft. Future & Halsey
"There's No Way" – Lauv Ft. Julia Michaels
"Exile" – Taylor Swift Ft. Bon Iver
"Positions" – Ariana Grande
"Bury a friend" – Billie Eilish
"Hold me while you wait" – Lewis Capaldi

AUTHOR'S NOTE

This is not a love story.
This is the beginning of the end.

Before everything, there was peace between the three most powerful crime families of Detroit city. The older generation came to an agreement to keep the peace between them, but now the new generation of the Holy Trinity rises and with it so does greed.

Once they were one and now lust, envy and greed poisoned their souls and corrupted their minds.

Let me take you back to where it all started and how everything went to hell between brothers, sisters, and friends.

This world I created has been an idea for so long, but I hope you enjoy this introduction to a new world of crime where the women are just as ruthless as the men or even more. I also hope that when you read the last page, you can't stop thinking about these characters, because I too am obsessed with them.

Note: This story takes place in the past. The next book in the series is set five years into the future after the events in Andrea "The Beginning". In this book you will get a glimpse of all the characters before they were Made. There is a brief torture scene mention of sexual abuse and a lot of foul language.

Proceed with caution.

What is the Holy Trinity?

The Holy Trinity is the most notorious crime organization in the United States of America. It is run by three crime families who joined forces after a war over Detroit City. They each rule over their own family but only one has full control of the entire organization. Currently the Nicolasi family has full control of the Holy Trinity. They reached an agreement with the other two crime families and handed over a small percent of the territory.

The Holy Trinity is composed of the Nicolasi, Volpe and Parisi family. The Nicolasi family deals in the gun trade, the Volpe family deals in the drug trade and the Parisi handle the more legitimate side of the organization including the casinos and strip clubs.

For years, the three crime families of Detroit City have ruled together in peace. Now the new generation rises and so does greed.

Man or woman it matters not.

Three will be chosen to be boss.

Only one of them will be crowned the Don.

WHO'S WHO IN THE HOLY TRINITY?

NICOLASI FAMILY

Benedetto Nicolasi (Boss of the Nicolasi family and head of the Holy Trinity)
Cassius Nicolasi (Benedetto's son)
Demetrio Nicolasi (Benedetto's son)
Andrea Valentina Nicolasi (17-18)
Lorenzo Antonnio Nicolasi (17)
Valentino Alexander Nicolasi (17)

VOLPE FAMILY

Tommaso Volpe (Boss of the Volpe family and underboss of the Holy Trinity)
Natalia Volpe (Tommaso's ex)
Lucan Tomas Volpe (18)
Giana Alexis Volpe (16)
Cara Mia Volpe (15)

PARISI FAMILY

Gabriele Parisi (Boss of the Parisi family, Consigliere of the Holy Trinity)
Arianna Luna Parisi (18)
Kadra Sofia Parisi (16)
Mila Areya Parisi (15)

You are never too old to set another goal, or to dream a new dream. – C.S. Lewis

PROLOGUE

"Life's full of tough choices, isn't it?"
- Ursula

Andrea

23 years' old
Wedding day

"YOU READY?

My father comes into my waiting room, I stand from the love seat and take a deep breath. His fierce blue eyes stared back at me with so much love and fear.

Fear for my life and for my future.

A future that is no longer mine.

"It's not too late to get you out of here sunshine, you don't have to walk down that aisle." My father says.

"I do have to." I whisper harshly. I do not mean to be rude but I'm losing it. My very own personal hell on earth will start in less than twenty minutes.

I knew this day would come; I was just too naive in thinking he would set me free. I thought that once I was out of his life, he would move on from the memory of me.

Of our short time together back in his territory. The Volpe boss still thinks of me as property, as a game. He did back then, and nothing has changed. Now he is proving it by taking away my peace, choice, and freedom.

He said he would get me back no matter the cost and now I am paying the price.

"You are fucking mine."

Even after all these years, those words still haunt me and so does his betrayal. I let my guard down around the devil and he didn't think twice before selling me out.

And now after all this time he kept his promise.

He found me and made me his.

Today on my wedding day there is nothing left of the Andrea Valentina Nicolasi that I used to be. The girl I used to be when I first met him.

I was strong but I was also foolish.

But he fucked with the wrong bitch. I am stronger and wiser now; I am no longer alone.

I have my family in my corner and the Volpe boss will wish he would have stayed gone and forgotten.

He threatened what I hold most dear to my heart.

That night five years ago, I left Detroit like a rat in the night because he conspired against me. He wanted me to go, so he set my entire world on fire and left me to deal with the burning chaos all on my own.

That was his task after all. Running me out of town and sending me back to my world. What he didn't know was that he sent me to hell, but I didn't go alone.

I had his son.

My prince.

Our boy.

A beautiful boy born of good and evil. So today I marry a liar and a cheat, just to protect my son from his father.

He can't know of his existence.

I look at my baby boy sitting quietly while drawing on the coloring book he loves so much, oblivious of the danger surrounding his very existence. Roman has the same light brown hair as his father but everything else is all me. My sweet boy is all me and all mine.

Nothing will ever threaten that.

I kept his existence a secret to keep him safe.

"You know I'll protect him with my life, Andrea. Nothing will touch him." my father assures me.

I was so lost in my head that I didn't notice my father's arrival. We have come a long way since the first time I met him five years ago. There isn't another man on this earth like him, who has been through what he has been through and still has risen above it all. He has proven himself to me and I forgave him. I don't trust anyone but him. I trust him with my life but most importantly with my baby boy. My son's father is not the only threat lurking in the shadows of my mind, there is something so much worse coming for me.

"I know you will." I need someone to protect my baby, even from myself. What if I end up like my mother? I shake off the dark thoughts and kiss my father one last time before I turn around and fix my veil. — "I'll make him regret what he did to me back then and what he's doing now." I smile at my dad while I put my hand through his arm.

It is time.

If he wants me, then he shall have me, but I'll bring hell on Earth and even the score. I almost lost everything five years ago because of his greed. I won't let him take anything else. *Not again.*

You might be wondering who I am, and which events led me to this god awful day.

The wedding from my nightmares.

Five years ago, I met the man I would soon call husband and he tried to ruin me.

He won't get another chance.

I take one last glance at my reflection; my black wedding dress is a mockery to the church and to the family's traditions. It is a declaration of war. They won't be pleased with it, but I am not afraid. I have come a long way since those dark days, and he doesn't know me anymore.

None of them do.

I am Andrea Nicolasi soon to be Volpe and this is the beginning of our end.

UNE

Welcome To The Family

"They can live in my new world or they can die in their old one."
– Daenerys Targaryen

Andrea

Seventeen years' old
One month ago.
Manhattan, New York

WHEN I WAS A KID, I USED TO LOVE WATCHING MY MOM get all dolled up. She was always the most beautiful woman in the room and the men would try to steal her attention. They'd do practically anything just to have her stunning honey-brown eyes on them, if even for just one second.

The women? They didn't quite vibe with my mother. My father used to say Valeria Turner's beauty could make any man fall to his knees. At least, that's what I think he used to say, I wouldn't really know. I never met the man, but my mama used to tell me all kinds of stories about him and their short-lived romance. To this day, I have doubts about those stories. It always felt like she was reciting one of those cheesy fairytale's parents tell their kids to give them a false sense of security. They hope for a happily ever after that will never come.

It's bullshit.

All of it.

This moment in time proves that fairytales don't exist, at least not for me. If fairytales were real, I wouldn't be here today. I wouldn't have this hole in my heart tearing my insides apart.

I look down at my mother, still as beautiful and regal as ever. Not a hair out of place and her makeup impeccably done. She is wearing her favorite dress; the red one she wore every year for my father's birthday. She'd put that damn dress on, make me sing happy birthday, and blow out the candles on a cake he would never eat. — *"Can you believe that?"* Even though he left her like she meant nothing, like we meant nothing. That was my mom, sweet as can be, even when life was the cruelest bitch to her. Her smile never faltered, not even once.

Until today.

Her stunning smile is frozen and cold, just like the useless organ in my chest that has caused me nothing but pain.

I reach out and touch her cold and frail hand. Nothing like the woman she was in life. My beautiful mother is trapped in this damn box and she's taking my heart and soul with her. I feel everyone's eyes on me, and it's making me sick. All she wanted was a private wake and the media turned this into a damn circus show. Not one of them knew her. Nobody knew the real Valeria Turner. To the world, she was a pretty face on a billboard, a body fit for their high fashion clothes, and one of the world's highest-paid supermodels. They all wanted something from her, maybe too much. I just wanted her smiles, hugs, and kisses. What I wouldn't give to have her back.

Oh, God. Please bring her back. — I finally let myself fall apart and cry over my beautiful mother and the future we'll never have.

I hear the whispers behind my back and the disrespectful sound of their cameras and smartphones clicking. I know they feel pity for the poor rich girl that just lost her mom, but they won't waste a second to post about it on social media or sell stories to gossip magazines.

They know nothing.

I've known loss from an early age, and I'm used to it. I lost my grandparents when I was only six years old and mom and I never recovered from that. I never had a father figure, so I didn't grieve the death of my father, but still, I wonder what could've been.

I wouldn't be an orphan today.

I wouldn't have to face all of this alone.

Yes, I know you might be thinking: "Bitch, you're an heiress of a multi-million-dollar fashion empire." Trust me a couple of millions in my name and the fame that comes with it, does not take the pain away.

Now, I only have my father's side of the family left. I have never met them, so it is obvious I can't count on them. Besides I don't want to be associated with them, but I don't have a choice. Mom told me all about them and how they're criminals hiding in plain sight.

Respectable citizens by day and monsters wearing Italian suits by night. *They never reached out to me before so why now? And why after mom is long gone? Is it because now I am at my most vulnerable?*

I'm so lost in my dark thoughts that I miss the distinct sound of the chapel's door opening announcing the arrival of guests. I turn around when I hear someone clearing their throat.

An immaculate older man is standing right in front of me. It's hard not to notice him as he has an air about him, a powerful persona you can't ignore—with jet black hair with some gray around the sides, intimidating eyes, and a full suit. He looks like a character straight out of a nineties mafia crime movie.

I'm still holding my mom's cold hand when he speaks the words that, although I knew were coming, still change my life forever. Emilio, my mother's most trusted friend, and business partner warned me this would be my fate for a couple of months. Since I am still underage, and my mother's side of the family is all gone, then the judge appointed my long-lost grandfather as my guardian. The worst thing? This man that I've never met and has never been part of my life holds my inheritance hostage.

Until I turn eighteen at least.

"I know you are hurting bambina, but it is time to come home. There's nothing left for you here." he says with finality. He came to my mother's wake and in the minute, he has been here not once has he looked in her direction.

I look into his cold eyes and can't shake the feeling of dread that runs through my whole body. "Who are you?" — with fake bravado I face the man that has never been a part of my life until today.

He offers me a smile that doesn't quite reach his eyes, before giving me his back and facing the goons dressed in all black that he brought with him today.

"I am Benedetto Nicolasi, but you can call me grandfather." The moment he announces himself, everyone begins to whisper.

The infamous Benedetto Nicolasi.

Current *Capo dei capi* of the three crime families of Detroit.

I close my eyes and let those words wash over me while I release the breath I've been holding ever since this man arrived.

My mother always warned me that one day her past would

catch up to her, and now it did. I bet she didn't account for her not to be here with me when it happened.

I can vividly hear her last words. "*Vida mia*, it's ok. Andrea... don't be scared. Trust me and be my brave girl." — her words settled down deep in my bones, fueling me with strength.

"Your father fought for us and went against his family and that was his undoing. The only way to survive them is by showing no weakness." — she tells me while looking into my eyes — *"Never bend to their will, be the queen in their game and fight sunshine. Fight like hell for your freedom and happiness. Promise me."* — she finished with conviction. I could feel her pain and torment on her deathbed worrying about the dark future that is waiting for me, promising nothing but pain.

I remember like it was just yesterday the night my mother finally revealed who my father was and what the Holy Trinity of Detroit means. I never imagine after all these years with no contact, my estranged criminal family would come looking for me.

Why now?

I kiss my mother one last time as one lone tear slowly falls on her cheek. I gently grab her cold hand and whisper so no one can hear. "I'll love you till the end of my days and even then, I will still love you, forgive me."

With one last look and a heavy heart, I say goodbye to my mom and the beautiful life we had. Her naive, trusting, and loving daughter is gone.

It is the only way to survive this new life without her.

I turn my back on my mother and face the stranger that calls himself my grandfather. Benedetto holds out his hand and offers a deceiving smile. "Welcome to the family, *cara mia*." I put my hand in his, hold my head up high and let him lead me to my new reality.

Detroit City.

Where the Holy Trinity awaits.

DUE

NEW WORLD

"People don't tell you who you are. You tell them."
– Serena van der Woodsen

Andrea

Now
Detroit, Michigan

NICOLASI.

That's what they call me now.

Andrea Valentina Nicolasi – Turner.

Back home, it was certainly chaotic with me being the only daughter of one of the most successful supermodels and fashion designers of the decade. Paparazzi followed my every move there, but here no one cares about me. I don't know what Benedetto did but there's not one single camera in sight.

Detroit.

I left New York City for this.

Unwillingly, but still, this sucks big time.

The suburbs are filled with uptight cheating assholes and desperate housewives; spoiled brats that think the world owes them something and, therefore, feel untouchable. I've been here three days and I already want to hang myself or stab my eyes out with a knife.

Whichever hurts less.

Dramatic but true.

Today, Benedetto, or grandfather, as he keeps reminding me, sat me down for a brief chat. He wanted to get to know me. I call bullshit. He had seventeen years to get to know his granddaughter, but he never bothered before, so the question is why now?

Why when I'm only a few weeks shy of eighteen and I will no longer be under his custody? I'll just have to endure this family until then.

He also wants to introduce me to everyone that is part of his circle of criminals. I don't care to meet anyone like I don't care to call him grandfather. I just want these weeks to fly by so I can be back in New York and continue my mother's legacy. I want to take Valentina Co. to new levels and add my own touch to it.

Still, I'm conflicted.

I want to leave this place as soon as possible but I also want to know what happened to my father. *Why did he break my mother's heart and abandon us?* Mom told me all about the Nicolasi family but never once told me exactly what happened to my father.

I can't leave this shit hole without knowing why my mom was so scared for me on her deathbed.

So, I'll play nice with them.

Keep your enemies close and all that shit.

I only have one ally right now and that's Emilio. He was there for my mother when everyone wanted to take advantage of her. He became her confidant and like an uncle to me. Benedetto oversees my inheritance, but Emilio is running Valentina Co. until I turn eighteen. When that time finally comes half of my mother's fortune will be in my possession and the other half is for my children. She always did want grandbabies. I sigh while picking up my phone and shoot Emilio a quick text. I need him to keep me updated on what's going on back in New York.

I look in the mirror and inspect my new hair. It's straightened almost to perfection and the new white-blonde highlights I added early this morning makes my honey brown eyes pop. It's freaky how much I look like mom today. She always told me I was her twin but we both knew that I only inherited the color of my eyes and slightly tan skin that comes from her Puerto Rican side. I love my mother's culture; it was a big part of my life when my abuela was alive. I know Spanish because my mother never failed to speak the language when it was just us. I am so proud of my Puerto Rican side. Our people are resilient, happy, and never fail to lend a helping hand. Although I was born here in the US, my mom and abuela never failed to teach me about the enchanted island in the Caribbean surrounded by only beauty and water.

Mom also taught me a little bit of Italian but only the basics because she was not fluent. She always repeated the few words my father taught her when they were together. Now that I am older, I am so grateful to her that she taught me to appreciate different cultures and because of it I am bilingual.

We are living in a world and in times where most people fear what's different or what they don't understand. Growing up when I slipped up and spoke Spanish people would tell me to go back to my country or to speak English because we are in America. I was young and I let their rude and discriminatory comments get to me to the point, there was a brief period where I only spoke English.

Mom also told me how a lot of people in the industry made her feel like she was inadequate or lacking when she talked in her native tongue. That's one thing I want to change about the fashion industry.

They judge what's different, what they don't understand and can't control.

But sadly, that's where our similarities ended. Nobody ever thought of us as mother and daughter. Since she gave birth to me when she was only eighteen years old, everyone mistook us for sisters. Mom told me once how she had to drop out of college because she couldn't work full time to provide for me and go to classes at the same time. So, she worked two jobs, as a salesgirl by day and a waitress by night. Although I can imagine it must've been hard, she never gave up.

She always fought for us.

For me.

Now it's my turn.

I step away from the mirror and turn on the tv, I still need to keep in touch with what's happening back in New York. See, when my mother died, it was all over the news. Everywhere I looked, news articles were speculating about her passing, trying to ruin her name. Instead of showing love and mourning her, the news and magazine outlets were reporting garbage, gossip, and speculations about her death. Hot Gossip magazine even wrote a piece about the future of my mom's company now that she is gone, but no one reached out to offer their condolences. How quickly she was forgotten and became old news. People only care about the current hot topic and selling their shitty magazine articles.

Sadly, that's how the world of the elite works.

My mother was so much more than a stunning face on a magazine cover. She was compassionate and was always giving back to the less fortunate, never asking for anything in return. I might be fashion royalty, but I wasn't raised like the airheads that live to flaunt their luxurious lifestyles pretending on the gram and living off of their daddy's money. I want to do more with my life, something meaningful.

I want to make her proud.

I turn the tv off and snap some quick selfies for my social media. I thought about hiding away and grieving but sadly I can't do that. In this industry, everyone knows who I am and that soon I'll be the new face of Valeria Turner's fashion empire. They'll expect certain things from me and over my dead body will I let my mom's dream burn to ashes or be stolen from me.

And I have a feeling my mom's fashion empire is the only reason Benedetto Nicolasi dragged me here after all these years.

I look at my reflection in the mirror one last time and I am proud that I look like her. Well, unless you count the new nose ring —a tiny diamond and the bloody red lipstick shade I'm wearing today.

Valeria Turner was always elegant and refined. She didn't need a lot of anything because she looked young and beautiful no matter what. She wouldn't be caught dead wearing red lipstick. Abuela taught her when she was young that red was the devil's shade. How ironic is it that red is my favorite color?

In all my baby pictures I am wearing something pink. Once I got older, mom let me experiment with my style and although she was a fashion icon and all eyes were on her, she never judged me and not once made me feel discouraged or afraid to express myself.

I remember this one time we attended Paris fashion week and I wore a black polka dot dress with green rain boots and

Minnie Mouse ears that she bought me the summer before when we went on a vacation to Disney World.

She was decked out in designer clothing and wearing her favorite black faux fur coat, looking like the bad-as-fuck fashion icon she was. And still, she proudly showed me off to the world and was never embarrassed of me. Not even once.

A lot of famous designers mocked her decision of not using dead animals for her designs, but she also gained popularity and more supporters because of her brave decision to break stereotypes and ignore outdated fashion traditions in those times.

I am my mother's daughter after all and now that I am here in Detroit surrounded by haughty and snobbish people, I don't really care to fit in.

I make my own damn trends and I would not be caught dead with the desperate housewife look.

Hell no.

I want to stand out and stand strong.

I move around my new room and feel a bit of nostalgia because the room is almost identical to the one I had back in New York. I appreciate the fact that they didn't order someone to make me a princess room all covered in pink.

Dammit, I can't escape this fucking color.

The walls are all white, with a huge bed covered in red satin sheets. In the corner of the room, there is a beautiful pearl white antique bookshelf filled with all my favorite books and next to it there's a desk with painting and drawing equipment. I don't know how they knew drawing is my passion, the only one that did was mom.

My room has a beautiful balcony covered in red roses with a perfect view of the mansion's entrance.

This is my dream room, the one I always wanted but was almost impossible to have since we lived in a penthouse with no garden view or balcony, the only view I had was the busy streets of Manhattan.

I find it strange that Benedetto knows that I love to read and that my passion in life is drawing. Only mom knows, well knew. With a heavy heart, I close the balcony's doors and walk to the closet. I need to choose what I'm wearing tonight; I need something that will give an 'I don't give a fuck' what you think statement.

There's a loud knock on my door that immediately interrupts my train of thought.

A guy I've never met before strolls in like he owns the place and sits on my bed. He's tall with jet black hair, blue eyes, and a wicked smile. He has a lip ring and a neck tattoo of a woman's eyes.

This guy doesn't look like all the other goons I have come across since I've been here.

So unusual.

A sinister smile resembling Cheshire cat spreads across his handsome face. Yeah, I must be careful with this one. Those with the prettiest smiles and kind eyes are the ones that usually stab you in the back with your own knife.

"So, the prodigal daughter has returned home." He smiles but there's nothing friendly about his condescending tone and I can feel the atmosphere change real quick. Benedetto has not introduced me to the family yet, but mom told me all about my dad's brother Cassius and his two sons, Valentino and Lorenzo Nicolasi. She never forgot to mention them, but always with a sad smile on her pretty face.

The dude is staring at me, waiting for a response. I can't give anything away, especially that I know of him, so I decide to act clueless. "Who are you?" I question while staring at him.

Show no fear, sunshine, they'll feed on it. Thoughts of my mother's last day consume my mind but in moments like this, it always gives me strength and a sense of calm so I can face anything and anyone.

I get out of my head and give this guy my undivided attention. *He's gorgeous. I have to admit that, but in a — I will give you the night of your life before I slit your throat and feed you to the dogs' kind of way and that's the type you need to stay away from.*

"Lorenzo Nicolasi, call me Enzo.", he stares at me for too damn long, like I'm a puzzle he needs to figure out and like he knows a secret I don't. "Cousin works too since we are family and all.", he winks as he gets off the bed walking towards me.

"Ok, cousin, mind telling me why you barged into my room?", by the annoyed look on his face, it's obvious he didn't miss the venom in my voice. He gets closer and from the way he's clenching his jaw, I can tell I pissed him off.

Good.

"I just wanted to meet my cousin, that's all." The way he says cousin feels wrong. He said it like it's a dirty word and it pains him. He is now toe to toe with me, and I have to raise my head to look at him. From this angle I have a better view of his unusual neck tattoo, there's a name around the woman's eyes, I can tell it ends with the letter 'A', but before I can take another look, he steps away from me. "See you later, cuz.", he regards me with a cruel smile before he turns to leave.

What...the...fuck.

How can someone change moods so quickly? It was like

having a conversation with two different people.

Dr. Jekyll and Mr. Fucking Hyde.

TRE

Cruel World

"After all there are things so much worse than death."
- Jafar

Lucan

YOU COULD SAY CARRYING THE NAME VOLPE COMES WITH many advantages. There's money, pussy, and power. My three favorite things in this fucked up world. I never wanted to be made, but I knew I could never escape it. My father made it clear that he does not agree with women leading men, so that leaves me as the only choice.

All my dreams and goals in life changed the moment he threatened my little sisters. If I dare to defy him and ignore my duty as the heir of the Volpe family, my girls will suffer the consequences.

And I'd do just about anything for them.

So, I learnt to enjoy it.

After the first taste of power, the savage in me was not satisfied, it wants more.

I fed the beast, but that's the problem.

It wants more to satiate the uncontrollable need for power.

Before, I never wanted to be king, but now I can't deny the

appeal. Everything I could ask for is thrown at my feet on a daily and I fucking love it.

But on days like today, I wish my mother would have taken me with her eight years ago when she left this place.

Detroit, Michigan

Our territory.

We run a third of this city. Everyone with the name Volpe, Parisi, and Nicolasi can do whatever they please and get away with it. Here, the children of the most notorious crime families in the United States of America are treated like royalty, as if we are untouchable.

We are and everyone knows it.

Nights like this one, where I have a warm body lying next to me, satisfied-as-fuck after three rounds of fucking — still don't manage to distract me from the fact that my mother ran away with her lover and never looked back. She just fucking left like we meant nothing to her. On this very same day eight years ago, she ran from the city and abandoned us.

This year her betrayal hurts a little bit less, but it's still there. Reminding me why I can't trust anyone, especially with what's left of my heart. If there's anything left that is.

Ring, ring, ring...

I already know who it is before I even check the caller ID. It must be serious if he's taking time out of his precious day to call me. He usually sends one of his dogs to fetch me.

Fuck.

I throw my head back and groan. I contemplate sending him to voicemail, but that never ends well for me. My father is one petty bitch and I always get stuck with the shit jobs when he's pissed with me and doesn't get his way.

I hit the green button and my father's commanding voice booms over the line. "Wake the fuck up, son. It is time." — There is a long pause before he continues. — "Demetrio's child has come home; you know what to do and if you fail...your sisters will pay the price for your mistake.", with that he ends the call.

I push the bitch off me and walk to the balcony. Tommaso's words replay in my head on a loop and taunt me. "Demetrio's daughter has come home."

Finally.

She's home.

"Come back to bed, baby," Cassia purrs. I need to stop fucking her, the bitch is getting greedy and I don't need this shit. I know she wants more, but I can't offer her anything but a quick and meaningless fuck. We established this before we started messing around, but she didn't get the memo and started running her mouth at the academy saying we are fucking exclusive.

"Get dressed and get out." I'm done with her anyway and I have more important matters to attend to.

She quickly gets dressed and heads out, but before the door closes, I hear her mutter under her breath.

"Asshole."

I ignore the insult because I know it's true. I never pretended to be anyone's knight in fucking-shining armor. This is who I am, and it is what it is.

A few minutes pass and I'm still replaying my father's words. The heir of the fallen Nicolasi has come home and the poor girl has no idea what is coming to her. The Volpe family won't ever accept a woman as the head of the Holy Trinity. That's one of the many things the three families disagree on. The Parisi have broken that stigma but the Volpe won't ever submit to a woman in command.

This is my only chance to prove that there's no better choice for capo than me. Tommaso will make my sisters pay the price for my failure if I don't prove myself and become the next Capo of the Holy Trinity.

I won't fail.

I can't.

Nicolasi may very well be the most powerful family of The Holy Trinity, but that doesn't guarantee them the title of the head of the three families. The Nicolasi, Volpe, and Parisi children are at war for the crown and only one of us will wear it.

Me.

I light up a joint while I throw my head back and close my eyes. "I'm sorry Ma." I exhale and offer the night sky a cold smile. I can almost hear her heartbreaking in the still, dead night. Well, the bitch left us like we never meant anything to her so fuck her.

Today, a piece of the boy my mother raised dies, and in his place? The monster, the savage, and the future fucking king comes out to play.

My father says I was born to rule over this cruel world.

My whole life I've been groomed to take Tommaso Volpe's place even when I didn't want to turn out like him but now there's no other choice and the time has come. No one will stop me and no one... fucking no one will take my crown.

Especially the bastard child of the fallen Nicolasi.

I will annihilate her.

There's no room for failure.

QUATTRO

You Can Call Me Lucan

"Wicked always wins."
- Zelena

Andrea

"MISS NICOLASI, THEY ARE READY FOR YOU NOW." I LOOK up from my computer just in time to watch Roberta, one of the maids, head out of my room. I shiver as soon as she's gone. She comes off as cold and honestly so rude. She also looks like the mean principal in that kids' movie that everyone was afraid of. You know the one that made the young child eat a whole damn chocolate cake by himself and grabbed the little girl by her braids, sending her flying across the schoolyard?

Yeah, that evil hag.

I study myself in the mirror one last time and I'm more than satisfied with the finished look. Benedetto specifically told me it would be a formal event. I'm sure they'll be mad at my choice in wardrobe but it's a good thing I don't care. These people need to understand that I won't abide by their rules or standards.

I'll always stay true to myself and although I love the glam life, I don't follow orders. I never have and I never will.

Once I'm done, I walk down the huge and elegant staircase

that leads to the main area where everyone is gathered. When I reach the last steps, I stop dead in my tracks because holy shit the place is packed with men in suits and women wearing expensive dresses. I look down at what I'm wearing. I chose a short and strapless black dress that stops mid-thigh. I paired it with a baggy jean jacket and some white sneakers. I didn't even try with my hair and makeup; I applied some mascara, a pink gloss and let my natural waves lose. I look like I do when I go out with my friends for a casual night out and nothing like the women that are in attendance tonight. My mother would've laughed her ass off if she was here to witness this spectacle.

The judgement and disapproval are visible in their Botox filled faces. They must think I'm not up to their standards and I don't deserve one second of their precious, pompous time. Mom taught me to never judge a book by its cover, but it doesn't take a genius to know that these people are obviously judging me. So, fuck them, their opinions of me will never keep me up at night. I'll show them I'm just as fucking lethal with my white chucks as I am with my red stilettos.

When I first arrived at the Nicolasi mansion, I didn't care enough to admire the place, but now while I walk down the staircase, I'm amazed by it all. The decor is white and black. There are expensive looking vases with candles all over the place, beautiful paintings, and modern furniture. It looks like something out of a home decor magazine. I knew these people were rich as hell, but damn I guess the criminal world really does pay off.

I'm almost to the last step when the cheesy music playing in the background stops and Benedetto meets me at the end of the stairs. He holds out his arm for me to take and squeezes it gently, but the warning is there.

Behave.

Huh. I guess someone isn't too happy with me right now.

Oh, well.

In one swift move, I find myself in the middle of the room with all eyes on me.

"Everyone, it is with great pleasure that I introduce to you my beautiful granddaughter, Andrea Valentina Nicolasi. I expect everyone to treat her like the princess she was born to be." Benedetto beams with pride as he acknowledges everyone in the room. But dear old grandpa, has one thing wrong though. I am not a princess, never was and never will be.

They'll learn that soon enough.

The crowd surrounding me parts and a man I only know from the photos my mom showed me, walks towards me. He is handsome no doubt, with his dark blond hair styled without a single hair out of place and deep soulless blue eyes the same shade as his asshole son. The man steps forward, grabs my hand, and lays the softest of kisses before introducing himself. "It's a pleasure to finally meet you, Andrea." His smile seems almost genuine. If I didn't know better, I would almost believe it. "I'm your uncle Cassius." Now that we are this close, I can smell a hint of alcohol in his breath.

There is something melancholic about Cassius. The blank stare he gave me a couple of minutes ago is gone and now there is only sadness. This doesn't fool me because I know for a fact this man is not innocent nor is, he to be trusted. The few times mom mentioned his name, a frown would appear on her gorgeous face.

When the moment feels extremely uncomfortable, I remove my hand from his grip and stare at his face. "The pleasure is all mine Uncle," I lightly dip my head and smile while lying through my teeth.

He offers me a knowing smile. "You have your mother's eyes." Before I can process his weird comment and ask him how he knows that mom and I share the same shade of honey brown eyes, when I know for a fact, they weren't that close. My mom rarely spoke about him. I didn't even know of his existence until a few years ago. I don't have the opportunity to do so because we are interrupted by his son.

Lorenzo, so inopportune.

I notice that there is something different about him tonight. He ditched his face piercings, traded in the reckless bad boy look for a more sophisticated look. He looks like he stepped out of an Armani fashion show. But wait, this guy has hair the color of snow. It takes me only a moment to realize that the guy before me is not Lorenzo.

It is his twin.

"By the surprised look on your face, I can tell you didn't know my boys are twins." Cassius points out.

Little does he know that there's not much I don't know about the Nicolasi family, but yes, the twin thing is a surprise. *Mom never mentioned twins.*

"I'm Valentino." Lorenzo's carbon copy steps forward. They're almost identical. The only difference is the color of their hair and Lorenzo's tattoos and face piercings. They are both incredibly handsome but in completely different ways. Lorenzo has the bad boy, rough around the edges look while Valentino has an air of regality about him. He also looks demented, like the kind of guy that will rip your heart out of your chest and stomp on it with his expensive Gucci shoes.

It was always unusual how strange mom acted every time

Cassius was mentioned. It was like she wanted to tell me more about him, but something always held her back.

All chatter dies down and everyone gives whoever walked through the doors their undivided attention. Well, finally I'm not the most interesting thing in the room.

I turn around and find myself staring at the most beautiful pair of clear blue eyes, so clear I can almost see my reflection staring back at me.

Huh.

I have always been proud of the fact that I never lose my cool when I'm around hot guys but damn this one is stunning. Even more handsome than my ex-boyfriend, the jerk that dumped me because "I wasn't fun anymore." *Well duh bitch, my mom just died.* I'm still a bit salty about his sudden but expected departure from my life once shit got tough.

This guy has perfect chiseled cheekbones, a straight nose and the lightest shade of brown hair slicked back without a single hair out of place. Longer on the top and short on the sides.

I've been around plenty of hot men before, but this stranger looks like a model and an MMA fighter all wrapped up in one sinful package. He is very attractive and by the arrogant smirk on his face, he knows it too.

With a swagger only guys like him possess he meets me halfway in the middle of the room and takes my hand in his before laying a quick peck on it.

A devious grin forms across his face as he looks me up and down. There's nothing friendly about the look he's giving me, that's for sure.

"Welcome to Detroit, *principessa*." That's all he says before releasing my wrist and turning to leave, but before he does, he looks over his shoulder at me. — "We are going to have so much fun together", he heads to the other side of the room and leaves me with that parting comment that feels a lot like a threat.

I need to be careful, it's obvious this one will bring me nothing but trouble.

Before he is completely out of reach, I realize he didn't tell me his name and for some unknown and inexplicable reason I need to know it.

"And who might you be?" My voice is strong and proud, but he doesn't even turn around to answer me. *What a douche.*

I'm about to call him out for being arrogant and damn rude, but before I do, he turns around and acknowledges me.

"You can call me Lucan and I'll be seeing you princess." He winks before he has the audacity to dismiss me.

I have never met a more arrogant guy in my entire life. The creep must think he is God's gift to mankind.

By our brief encounter I am sure I'll be seeing him again and it won't be pleasant. There was nothing friendly about him.

Shit.

I can't be making enemies here. I'm out of my element but if he thinks he can mess with me or intimidate me.

He is dead wrong.

Whatever these people throw at me, I will survive.

They won't break me.

They can try but they won't succeed.

Never.

CINQUE

Holy Trinity Academy For Jerks

"You can tell a lot about a person by their shoes."
- Hannah Marin

Andrea
Two days later

I'VE BEEN GAWKING AT THE HUGE PRETENTIOUS BUILDING before me knowing that this day will be crap. It's nothing like Eastside River High, my school back in New York. Mom wanted me to be as normal as possible, so she made me go to public school and interact with all kinds of people, not just the rich and the famous. There is nothing normal about this academy. The front doors have a huge replica of the academy's crest. A crown, a burning cross, and the name of the three founding families, including mine. *How very religious and humble of them*. I roll my eyes as I reach for my class schedule. The twins left me behind and didn't even bother to give me a ride to the academy. I didn't expect them to.

I'm on my own here.

I put a stop to the pity party going on in my head. I hear murmurs all around me, so I lift my head up and stare at everyone surrounding the Holy Trinity academy's grounds. I notice there are some kids staring openly at me. It seems like they already made their minds up about me.

Must be the fact that I didn't put effort into my appearance today. I look like I don't belong and quite frankly that's the look I was going for. I really do hate this uniform. Black high heel boots, black mini skirt, a white shirt, and a gold tie. I look like the people that I dislike so much in this world, the rich and brainless. Besides, there's nothing stylish about it.

The high-end fashionista in me just died a little bit inside.

I'm almost to the academy's entrance when I notice laughter behind me. I turn around and see three exact replicas of Barbie staring at me like I'm the dirt beneath their ugly black boots. *Jesus, it's like staring at botched Barbie times three.*

Look I have nothing against plastic surgery. When the time comes that I might need some, I'll feel no shame in getting procedures done. My boobs will never meet my belly button. However, if you're doing something to your face, at least pay for a good doctor. It looks like the plastic surgeon was drunk or high during their procedures and fucked them up. That's what these girls look like.

How tragic.

"Hey, aren't you Valerie Turner's daughter?", a rude and snobbish voice interrupts my thoughts.

"Yeah, I am." I look her straight in the eye, so she knows she's not capable of intimidating me.

Not now, not ever.

I feel her judgmental gaze from head to toe, a look of disapproval on her face. – "You look nothing like her," she tells me, while I hear her friends snicker behind her.

I won't lie and say that didn't sting. My mother used to tell me that I was her mini-me and I took pride in that. I know this girl is being catty, so I won't let her wannabe Regina George ass get to me. It hurts but I'll never let it show.

I hold my head up high and smile. "And you look like the ugly Kardashian," I tell her. "You should really consider changing up your plastic surgeon, darling." I add the snarky remark before I give them my back and reach the academy's entrance.

I don't miss the outraged gasps behind me, and it is truly satisfying.

That'll teach them that I'm not one to mess with. I have bigger issues than worrying about what three blonde idiots think about me and my appearance.

"That was epic.", I hear someone say beside me. I turn and come face to face with a beautiful, short and curvy girl with black her hair in tight space buns. This girl has black lipstick on, and she makes it work. Not a lot of people can pull it off.

"You should really teach me your bitchy ways," she says while laughing at the three blondes that are sending death glares our way.

She ignores the girls and turns my way. "I'm Fallon Alicia James, lover of all things Marvel and hater of all things plastic." She holds out her hand for me to shake and I laugh at her choice of words.

This strange but stunning girl is hilarious and what makes her even funnier is her Captain America's socks that ruin the whole preppy and pretentious look of the academy's uniform.

I shake her hand and introduce myself. "I'm Andrea, cute socks by the way," I tell her. She beams at me, but in a flash, her whole expression changes and a frown appears on her pretty face.

Fallon stares at me with a serious look. "I just have one

question for you." she tells me.

"Shoot." I respond all the while trying to hold back a snort. In some weird way I feel like I've known this girl my entire life.

"Kourtney or Kim?", she asks, looking at me like our entire three-minute relationship depends on my answer.

"Uhm, I don't really follow them," I answer truthfully. I really don't follow them at all. I only know that they're famous for being naked and dating ballers and because once in a while they would ask for my mom's latest collection.

She's staring at me with a dumbfounded look on her face like she doesn't believe me. "Look, I don't really follow them, sorry." I guess there goes the only chance I had of a real friendship in this hell hole.

Fallon offers a wicked smile and holds the front door of the academy open for me. "I think I've met my soulmate." She says and pulls me in for a quick hug.

I hug her back and think that maybe, Holy Trinity won't be so bad after all.

Once I step inside Holy T's, I can't believe what I'm seeing. This place looks like all those pretentious and self-centered academies rich parents send their bratty kids to be "reformed" when they're too busy to do it themselves.

"Welcome to Holy Trinity Academy for Jerks." Fallon laughs at my bewildered expression all the way to my first class.

SEI

Boys Like Him

"Life is tough Serena. Just get a helmet."
- Blair Waldorf

Andrea

VOLPE.

During lunch break my new shadow, Fallon, gave me a brief summary of everything I need to know about Holy Trinity Academy. She explained that the academy has three founding families. The Volpe, Parisi, and not surprising at all...the Nicolasi family. It is surreal to witness how much power my father's side of the family holds in this city.

The Nicolasi name is notorious for being one of the wealthiest families in the country but also because of the rumors. The news outlets are always reporting about the great Benedetto Nicolasi and the rumors about the family dealing in criminal activities and how they launder the money to make it seem like their businesses are legit but also to fool civilians into thinking they're respectable people. What I was not aware of is that they shared control over the city with two other crime families. Apparently, a lot of Made Men fell during a war over Detroit territory and the three families came to an agreement to share the city but under the control of the Nicolasi family. I know all of this because my mother shared a lot during her last days with me, but I also did my homework before crossing over to enemy territory.

My mother used to say, "Don't play their games sunshine, play them." She knew what she was talking about too. She had nothing when she had me, just a broken heart and a three-month-old baby. She started as a salesgirl at one of Manhattan's most influential fashion boutiques. From there, she was discovered by a modeling agency and the rest, as they say, is history. Mom used to tell me how a lot of people tried to sabotage her and her brand, but she always played it smart and was graceful.

"Don't ever let them drag you down to their level, my love, it's quite filthy there." she would remind me.

A loud bang right next to where I'm standing interrupts the sad memories that consume me every time, I let my mind wander to thoughts of when she was alive.

The loud noise was caused by three guys that I don't know all that well but my first impressions of them was...well shit.

Right next to my new locker, the guy that I've met at the gathering, Lucan I think that's his name, is holding some kid by the throat, all the while my twin cousins stand by and let it happen. The dude is sobbing so embarrassingly loud that everyone stops what they're doing to witness the confrontation between the four of them.

Fallon told me that she moved from California to Detroit when she was a sophomore, but for personal reasons she went back to California in the middle of the school year. Now, she's back for senior year and she's spilling all the hot tea regarding Lucan's reign of terror in this place. She told me how everyone bows down to him and the female population falls on his dick every chance they get.

I found out he is the captain of the chess club. I would have never pegged him for the chess-playing type. Chess players need to develop a high degree of discipline to learn and play the game. Lucan seems like the type of guy that loves control, I guess that's why he enjoys the game. What does surprise me is the fact that he is Holy Trinity's student body president. I don't see him caring about anything other than himself, but maybe I'm just being a judgmental bitch. *Who knows?*

"I didn't do it, man, you have my word." I hear the kid's frantic shouts. There's something about the way he's acting that screams guilty to me.

Lucan slaps him across the face and laughs loud enough to attract the attention of more students. "Like your word means shit." He slaps him hard across the face again and the kid sobs louder.

Jesus, this is sad to watch.

Lucan steps away from the kid and Enzo takes his place. Grabbing the kid by the throat and shoving his head back into the wall of lockers. Lorenzo asks: "Did you do it, you sick fuck?" he shouts. Not caring that he's making a scene in the middle of the hall. "You're just making it worse for yourself, you're dead anyway bitch, so just admit it and let's be done with it."

If I were a different type of girl, I would step forward and help this kid, but the crazed look in his eyes makes me believe he's guilty of whatever they're accusing him of.

Suddenly there's a buzz inside my blazer's pocket. Emilio is calling me, but I send it straight to voicemail. I'll return the call later, I'm sure it's nothing urgent.

I shove my phone back into my pocket and start to move

when I stumble into the waiting arms of an asshole.

Shit.

"Did you enjoy the show *principessa*?" —Lucan whispers in my ear as he corners me until my back hits a wall. — "Did it get your nice and wet?", he says mockingly. The pig must think his dirty words have any effect on me.

"Nah, three against one fights don't really impress me." I sass. I hear Fallon snort in the background.

A locker slams shut, and the kid runs past us like his life depends on it, I guess it does.

"Yo, Volpe, catch you later." From my peripheral vision I see Lorenzo grab some random girl and take off like he was not just threatening another student's life just a minute ago.

The students clear the hallway and move on as if nothing ever happened. Only Valentino and Fallon remain, well besides Lucan.

I completely ignore him and take out the books for the next class, which is English literature. I'm already late and it's my first day.

Oh, what a great first impression that will make.

I was too busy trying to ignore Lucan that I almost missed the way my cousin Valentino looked at Fallon with so much animosity, as if he loathes the simple fact that she breathes the same air as him. There is definitely something going on between those two and by the looks of it, nothing good.

A man clears his throat, and it serves as an excuse to leave and avoid another second of this awkward exchange between my new friend and my cousin.

The someone that cleared his throat as a warning is my new lit teacher. "Do you like wasting people's time, Miss Nicolasi?" How nice. There are four students here and he felt like singling me out.

"I suggest you all head to your respective classrooms if you don't want detention for the next three Saturdays. Move along now." My new teacher stands there waiting for everyone to clear the hall.

Valentino is the first to move, quickly disappearing to his first class of the day while Fallon waits for me outside the door of the class we share.

I start to follow her when Lucan blocks my path with a smirk that promises retribution.

Mom always warned me about boys like him, the ones that hide their evil intentions behind a wicked, sinful smile.

She fell for one of those and look at what it got her, a bleeding heart, and a broken mind.

This is going to be a long-ass day.

SETTE

EVIL

"You call it 'pepper spray.' I call it bitch repellent."
– Regina Mills

Lucan

ALL MY LIFE, I'VE BEEN RESPECTED BY EVERYONE AROUND me. At an early age, grown men knew one day they would answer to me. At first, they feared the consequences of fucking with the Volpe heir and as I got older, they feared what I had become.

Tommaso Volpe's son.

The feeling of making others bend to my will is exhilarating and addictive.

I thrive on it.

I was high on that feeling when I was beating the absolute shit out of Logan Beauregard, that sick fuck. He thought he could get away with hurting our girl and he wouldn't suffer the consequences of the atrocious act he committed against one of our own. I wasn't planning on confronting him with so many witnesses around, but he provoked me and fuck it I couldn't hold myself back.

He will get what's coming to him.

The look on Andrea's face while I was beating the absolute

shit out of Beauregard, was something I was not expecting. The bitches in this place tend to shy away from danger when shit gets too real for them. They want to tame the bad boy until they come face to face with the sick and deprived man. Not the Nicolasi *principessa*. I could see the disgust written all over her gorgeous face, but I also saw a hint of excitement and curiosity in her eyes.

I can't ignore the fact that there's something about her that calls out to every dark part of me, bringing out every twisted and animalistic instinct that I possess. Andrea is no pushover, unlike every other bitch inside these halls. She's hot as fuck too and that's a problem for me.

The first time I saw her, she was wearing a short black dress and a too big for her jean jacket that hid all her curves. The outfit was a big fuck you to the families and although it pissed me the fuck off how she disrespects us in our own city, at the same time all I wanted was to push her against the wall in front of everyone and fuck her until she learned her place. One thing I learnt about her in our brief, but memorable encounter is that the Nicolasi *principessa* hides behind sarcastic remarks and all that sass. She can hide all she wants, but I see her. The darkness lurks behind that picture-perfect smile that does not quite reach her honey brown eyes.

I stand back and watch as she grabs her books and heads for her next class with Fallon. I need to talk to Val. I don't know what he's thinking and feeling after seeing Fallon for the first time in two years. He completed his task and now she's back in town.

I follow them without being noticed. For some unknown reason, I can't get enough of this girl.

I need to stop this before it's too late, but I can't help myself.

I need more of her.

She's just a job.

She's just a fucking job.

Andrea

I TAKE MY SEAT IN THE BACK OF THE CLASSROOM AS THE three dumb blondes strut through the door.

Of-fucking-course.

They move to sit next to me but end up swiftly turning towards the other side of the room. I look behind me and find Lucan staring them down.

It baffles me that people really do fear him. Yeah, he might be intimidating to some, but to me, he is just some entitled rich kid with a superiority complex.

He chooses the empty seat behind me. I can feel his gaze on the back of my head. He's almost breathing down my neck.

As soon as the class begins, the teacher wants everyone to go ahead and introduce themselves to the rest of the class.

One of the botched blondes goes first.

I think Mr. Gonzalez called her Cassia.

She goes on and on about herself and what she did for the summer. I'm having trouble staying awake and paying attention.

From the looks of it, so is the teacher.

About ten minutes pass before she's finally done and it's my turn to introduce myself to the class.

I rise from my seat and face my new classmates, all the while avoiding making eye contact with the devil himself. I'm used to this, so I'm not nervous at all. *Just say some basic info about yourself*

Andrea and sit down. That is it.

"My name is Andrea, but some call me Drea and I just moved here from New York and ..." I get interrupted by an annoying, nasally voice. "Didn't your mother just recently die?"

My heart sinks.

I witnessed firsthand just how these kids are assholes, but this is just evil.

"How about you shut up Cassia, before those pictures you so nicely sent me, end up in the hands of everyone you know." The last person I would imagine coming to my defense, just did. By the look of confusion on everyone's faces, I'm not the only one surprised by his actions.

I notice Lucan staring at her with nothing with disgust written on his face. I'm pretty sure if looks could kill, this Cassia chick would be dead and buried six feet under by now.

She stares back at him with betrayal written all over her face, but she gets the message and shuts up.

However, the damage has been done.

"Umm, yes, who's next?" Mr. Gonzalez nervously asks the class.

I take my seat and my face turns to stone; I don't want them, nor do I need them to know that her words wounded me just like she intended. I can handle their snarky remarks and bitchy attitudes, even comments about my appearance and how I'm a bastard. I can endure anything, except catty remarks about mom. Her rude question reminds me that my world is gone and buried.

"Hey there rainbow, smile.", she would always say that when I was sad. She'd tell me time and time again that I brought color to her dark days.

I can still hear her sweet voice in my head, but it does nothing to ease the pain.

She took all colors from my life when she left

OTTO

Away Fighting Dragons

"You don't do the right thing for a reward. You do it because it's right." – Mr. Gold

Andrea

MY MIND KEEPS REPLAYING MY FIRST DAY AT THE academy. Not one thing went my way. *Okay, I'm being dramatic.* Fallon happened, and I am so grateful that I met her. She's the real deal, that one. I'm glad I met someone somewhat normal in that place where half the student body population seems brain dead.

Well, she is normal by my standards.

She is also down to earth, smart, and, well I just love her sarcastic nature and dark sense of humor.

Other than her, there is nothing remotely pleasant about my time in the academy. None of the classes interest me, the teachers seem intimidated by teen assholes with money, and my classmates? All self-centered, narcissistic brats that only care about their appearance and their lavish lifestyles.

I should not be so harsh, but after what that brainless botched Barbie said about my mother in class, I have every right to be a judgmental bitch.

I'm currently writing our first paper for Lit class. Mr. Gonzalez asked us to write a five-page paper on our most prized possession. He was mad after the scene Cassia, Lucan and I caused in the middle of his class, so he gave us the assignment as punishment.

I'm almost done with the paper about my most prized possession, my mother's necklace. She gave it to me before she died, and I treasure it dearly.

There's a knock at the door just a second before Benedetto announces himself.

It's strange because in the week we've been living under the same roof, he has never come up to my room.

"May I come in, *cara mia*," it's so weird that such kind and polite words come out of this ruthless and deceitful man.

"Sure, go ahead," I reply. I cannot for the life of me figure out his intentions. Sometimes I feel like he genuinely wants me here but other times I feel like I'm just a pawn in a sick twisted game.

Benedetto takes a seat on the love seat next to my bed. "I know this is a difficult transition for you, but you'll learn to love it here," he tells me leaving no room for argument.

I stay quiet because what can I say? He must know I am not staying here for long.

God, this is so awkward.

I don't know this man.

"You remind me so much of him," —he says while looking at me, with a small smile on his face. — "*Mio figlio.*" My son.

I only know a few words in Italian and *mio figlio* is one of the few I understand.

"My dad?" I ask. "I don't know much about him, just the stories my mom used to tell me." I face him. "Will you tell me about him?" I genuinely want to know more about the mystery that is my father. I can't leave this place without at least knowing more about the man that broke my mother's heart and consequently broke mine when he left us. Mom never showed me a picture of him and there were none around our house. It was like she was keeping him all to herself. I never really understood why she made the decision to keep him a secret, but I trusted my mother blindly, so I never questioned her choices.

"Your father was always an inquisitive and fearless child. *Il mio bambino* was always getting into trouble and almost gave me a couple of hundred heart attacks when he was growing up."– he chuckles and I can see the love he feels for my father, just by the adoring look in his eyes. He opens an old journal and hands me a photo of a small child. The small child looks a lot like Uncle Cassius. The same blonde hair and big blue eyes. The kid is frowning at whoever is behind the camera.

Yeah, that's definitely Uncle Cassius.

He was a cute kid, even now he still looks the same as in this picture. "Why are you showing me a photo of Uncle Cassius?" I ask.

He chuckles. "No, *mia cara*, this is your father, Demetrio." Benedetto says.

He notices the shocked and confused expression on my face and frowns. "You did know your papa was Cassius's twin, didn't you?"

That's why mom never showed me a picture of my father. He had a twin. I don't get why she would keep this a secret from me.

"Ah, no." I shake my head and clear my thoughts, before continuing. "This is the first time I see a photograph of my dad."

Benedetto frowns and hands me the photo. "Keep it. He would want you to have a piece of him." I take the photo from him and stare at it.

As much as I try to hide it, my father's abandonment still hurts like hell. The little girl in me that used to keep the letters he used to send my mother under her pillow and told her friends that her dad was away fighting dragons. That girl is broken because as much as my mom filled my life with magic and love, there was one hole in my heart she could never fill. That hollow part of me was blindly waiting for her father to fix it, to love her.

Now it is too late. I not only lost my mother, but I also lost a father without ever really having him.

Benedetto keeps telling me stories about my father and I see a part of him I didn't see before. Yeah, he's the boss of three families and a businessman, but today I saw the father. A father who has buried his wife and his beloved son. A son he clearly loved more than life itself. I don't know why he doesn't talk with this kind of love about Cassius and the twins, but I'll find out soon.

He gets up from the love seat and heads for the door, before he turns to leave, I ask him: "Do you think, umm, you can tell me more about my dad? Maybe, another day?" I don't trust him and I'm sure he's hiding something from me.

"Sure, *bambina*. I would love to." — he smiles but it doesn't reach his eyes. – "Oh, before I go, your cousins suggested a get together with kids your own age to celebrate your arrival. It will be nice for you to meet the Volpe and Parisi, children.", he looks at me while I suppress the urge to roll my eyes.

I highly doubt Lorenzo is the type that suggests gatherings and especially not in my honor.

Something I am sure of; this night will end with me suffering public humiliation.

I won't let them break me, I won't. That is something I just can't afford to do.

"I would love that, grandpa." I intentionally call him that. It'll be easier for me here if I just pretend — "Can I invite a friend?", I add.

"Of course, *bambina*, have a good night." He smiles at me before he leaves the room and closes the door gently behind him.

I won't let myself care about anyone in this house, because the moment I let myself feel like I belong, life shows me in the cleverest and most painful ways that I do not. I'll save myself another heartache and keep my walls as they are, unbreakable.

Where no one can hurt me or worst...leave me.

NOVE

SICK FUCK

"A man unwilling to fight for what he wants deserves what he gets." – Killian Jones

Lucan

"YOU KNOW, BEAUREGARD, I REALLY DISLIKE BEING LIED to." I dig the knife deeper into the skin of his left thigh. I must give the bitch credit, I thought he would have pissed himself or passed out by now, but no the sick fuck won't break.

He will.

They all break.

It is just a matter of time.

After our confrontation in the halls at the academy, he got a taste of what was waiting for him once we got him alone. Before he left the academy's ground both Lorenzo and I grabbed him before he could run back to his crooked father. Now, Valentino has joined us in an abandoned warehouse, right outside the city where the family does most of the tortures and killings.

No one will hear him here.

"Tell me what you want. You want money? Is that it? My father can—"

"We don't want nor do we need your filthy money." I hand the bloodied knife to Enzo; he's been waiting for this.

It is his turn now.

"Dude come on that slut asked for it. She even screamed fo— Before he could get out another word, Lorenzo grabs an old rope from the table and ties it around his neck. — "Oh god, wait no, listen to me, it was all her—." Tired of his annoying voice, I shove a rag in his mouth.

His bullshit lies fall on deaf ears. He's been calling out to the devil for far too long and now he gets to see him.

I motion for Valentino to help me pick him up until he is standing on the chair while Enzo finishes tying the rope around his neck.

I enjoy this part the most.

It is Val's turn to choose how our prey dies. Last time was messy-as-fuck since Lorenzo lives for blood and torture. His twin brother does not.

Valentino abhors messes.

He volunteers to clean the murder scene every damn time. Now, he was appointed the cleaner of the three families.

The fucking neat freak.

Logan Beauregard's whimpers are grating on my last nerve.

The little bitch is crying uncontrollably now; he knows he'll meet his maker soon. Lorenzo likes it when they cry and fight until the end. Until they realize the end is soon coming and they won't be able to escape us.

Killing gets this idiot hard.

I will never admit this to anyone and quite frankly I rather choke on my own blood than admit it to Lorenzo. He is the best choice for capo, because unlike him I don't enjoy killing and torturing. I only do it because it is my duty and I have no other choice, but Lorenzo does. He loves coming up with new and creative ideas to make our enemies suffer before he sends them to hell.

Unlike his brother, Enzo lives for the bloodshed and chaos.

Logan Beauregard fucked up and there is no point in allowing him to explain himself. He knows he did it, but most importantly we know he committed the crime.

Valentino hacked into Beauregard's computer and found evidence that proved him guilty. He not only raped a girl, but he taped himself during the act and kept it so he could later get off while watching it. And the piece of shit uploaded the video to a fake social media account and now everyone will be able to witness her shame. The families did all they could to have the video taken down but still the internet is forever, and it is almost impossible for us to get rid of it completely.

The bitch was dumb enough to film himself while committing one of the sickest acts someone could ever do against another human being.

Look I'm no saint, trust me, some might call me sick too, but we have a code that we abide to.

We don't hurt innocents.

Fucking ever.

We are the judge, jury and executioner of this city and this bitch was found guilty on all accounts.

He not only raped a sixteen-year-old. He hurt a teenage girl that means something to us.

From the corner of my eye, I watch Valentino grab his phone before he takes some pictures. He likes to keep photos of our victims.

Lucifer worked extra hard on the twins.

They're sick as fuck.

I get close to the chair that is holding the rapist's weight and get in his face. "Say hello to Satan for us, I hope he fucks that ass up." With those last words, I signal Lorenzo to end it.

With a giddy smile on his face, he pulls the chair out from under him.

The drop is not high enough, so the impact doesn't break his neck. Beauregard falls on the floor. He is struggling for air while shaking uncontrollably. It is the way the body reacts when air is not reaching the brain.

I should let him die.

I really should.

Nothing would give me greater pleasure than ending him for the sins he committed against one of ours.

Reluctantly, Lorenzo cuts the rope and removes it from his neck just before this asshole loses unconsciousness. We don't get to decide when and how the motherfucker leaves this fucked up world.

She does.

With one last look at Logan Beauregard, we head out the door and leave him struggling for air on the dirty floor.

Like the dirty cockroach he is.

No one fucks with us and gets to live to tell the story. When his time comes, and it will, he will wish he would have died at our hands.

She will have her revenge.

Wait till he feels the pain of her wrath.

The dumb fuck has no idea the monster he created and what he unleashed upon this world.

DIECI

PHOENIX

"I think I might kill someone tonight."
– Monica Geller

Kadra

I WAKE UP FROM THE DEEPEST SLEEP I'VE HAD IN YEARS. Not one nightmare invaded my sleep. It didn't because my nightmares became my reality.

The one thing that no human should ever go through… happened to me.

My choice was taken away from me.

I was degraded and humiliated in the most horrible of ways. Still every single bone in my body aches because almost a day ago I lost my innocence in the most brutal of ways at the hands of a sick sadistic asshole.

I should have seen this coming.

While in no way what happened to me was my fault, my brain doesn't seem to comprehend that. I keep replaying that night over and over again until I lose sleep. Those memories cause the need to rub my skin clean until it hurts. Until I get rid of the feeling of his disgusting hands running forcefully down my body.

I can still smell him on me.

God, it feels like he will always haunt me.

I hate that I let Arianna manipulate me into going with her to Logan's end of the winter school term bash. If I would have just stayed home like I originally planned to, this would have never happened.

I wouldn't be going through this. Nothing bad ever happens when I stay in the dark. The demons that hide there never hurt me. Only humans do.

God, I've never felt this weak and vulnerable before. Even if by some miracle of God, I erased those horrible memories from my brain, everyone has seen my shame. Everyone at Holy Trinity has seen the video and they won't let me forget.

Their gossip is my pain.

Grandma Parisi used to say that humans are not born evil, they are made evil. That everyone has good in them. I never believed that before.

Until now.

She was right.

I was not born evil; I was made and there's nothing good left in me.

He took everything until there was nothing but rage and pain within me. Nothing but the hollow shell of the girl I used to be.

I was a stupid and naive girl that believed for once someone would choose her instead of her larger-than-life sister.

I was her task.

This is all her fault.

Arianna has always done what's best for her and fuck everyone else. Mommy's perfect little doll. She's nothing but a puppet.

Always has and always will.

There's a soft knock on my door. It has to be one of my sisters since my parents have not bothered to deal with me since this happened. Gabriele did what he always does when something happens to any of us, he blamed it all on me. My mom on the other hand can't even look at me without breaking down into a fit of rage and hysteria because of what people in our social circle might say. It's always about what others might think or say about us that concerns her.

Not the fact that I was almost beaten to death and raped on camera by a sick bastard that runs in our circle. No, mommy doesn't care about that. Just like Arianna, mom only cares about herself.

The noise on the other side of my door keeps getting louder but I don't want to see anyone. I don't want them to see me this way, but I am too tired to tell them to go away. So, I just stay in my head and don't pay whoever is outside my door any mind. If I just stay in my head, no one can hurt me there.

"Kadra..." Arianna, of course. "I wanted to see how you are—" I don't let her finish her sentence because I don't need or want her fucking pity.

"What? How am I feeling after your disgusting bitch of an ex raped and defiled me? How am I feeling after my shame was broadcasted all over social media because of you?" I don't care if she feels guilty and wants to ease her conscience by pretending to care. She never did before now, so she can shove her fake apologies.

"Oh God, Kadra don't you blame me for this. What happened to you was not my fault!", she raises her voice at me for the first time since we were little.

"That's where you are wrong big sis. The entire time he was forcing himself into my body, he was calling your name. He told me how he was tired of your games, that you are a cock tease, so he was settling for me." A piece of me dies little by little, every time I remember his words.

She sucks in a deep breath. She probably wants to say something but doesn't know what to say. My sister never shows emotions, that's why everyone calls her the ice queen. She doesn't care about anything or anyone unless it benefits her.

I laugh darkly at the broken look on her devastatingly beautiful face. For the first time, my sister is speechless and doesn't know how to react.

Maybe it is not her fault, she didn't make him do it but still, I am condemning her. I have always suffered the consequences of her actions and I am fucking done. That little girl with her head in the clouds that worshipped her sister is gone. Arianna's indifference towards Mila and I used to hurt, she is just like papa.

"Kadra," she begins, but I shake my head.

"No, don't even bother. I will only say this once because after tonight. I don't ever want to discuss this again and especially not with you. Any love or respect I felt for you is dead. After tonight I won't love you anymore and I think we both know you never really cared about us. Not really. I won't forgive you either. You knowingly ripped my life apart. Our family might forgive you, but my hatred is one consequence you will have to live with forever."

She nods, clearly holding back whatever she feels like she needs to say to defend herself against my accusations.

I don't fucking care anymore. Let her die a little bit more inside every time she remembers my words. "Now get the fuck out of my room, I am done with you.", I turn my back on my sister and I have not one ounce of guilt.

She stays rooted in the same spot for a couple of seconds before I hear the door click shut.

There's another soft knock on my door but the person doesn't wait for my consent before they come in.

"For fuck sakes, can't you all live me the fuck alone?" I'm so tired, I just want to go away, but they won't let me breathe.

"Kadra, I had a nightmare, can I come in?" the sweet and scared voice of my baby sister Mila is what does it.

I can actually feel my heart breaking until there's nothing left.

I lift my head up and stare at my *stellina*, Mila. My beautiful baby sister with a heart so big and a smile that could brighten anyone's world.

Not mine.

Not anymore.

I wish I could open my arms and protect her from her nightmares but I am too broken so I do the one thing I promise I would never do.

I turn my back on my little star.

It could've been her; she could have been raped and defiled and she wouldn't have survived this. The families already believe she is damaged goods, even when that's so far from the truth.

Mila is the heart of this family and nothing, not even what I am going through could hurt me more than seeing the light fade from my baby sister's eyes.

Time seems to slow down as we stare at one another. Dad would sell us to the highest bidder. Mom is a conceited puppet that does whatever he says and Arianna? We could never really count on her. *So, who will protect us now?*

"Kadra, are you feeling okay?", she whispers so softly, that for a moment I think I imagined it.

"Get out Mila, you can't count on me anymore." My voice is eerily calm and evil.

Mila's chin wobbles and tears gather in her pretty eyes.

I did this.

I am breaking her beautiful heart.

Logan might have broken my spirit, but I just broke my own heart.

She nods her head in defeat before turning to leave.

I feel the urge to stop her, to tell her that I don't mean it, that I am just hurting right now.

That I need her, but I stop myself before I do.

I need to keep her safe.

The old Kadra won't be able to do it.

Once she closes the door behind her, I finally give in and cry until there are no more tears left.

No one will ever hurt me again.

No one will ever get a chance to hurt my Mila.

They'll all bleed before that happens.

Everything hurts as I try to stand and walk to my mirror. I look like death. My hair hasn't been brushed in a day, my body is covered in bruises and I still have blood under my nails from when I tried to scratch him to get him off me. It was useless, he was stronger than me.

Even when it hurts to do so, I stand tall and look at the broken reflection staring back at me.

And just as the Phoenix rose from the ashes, I too will rise.

Everyone that had a hand in hurting me will pay.

They will all pay.

I never wanted to be the Parisi boss. I figured like everything else in life, the title would go to Arianna, but while I was being abused in the most painful of ways, I only had one thought.

This would've never happened to me if I was in control. If I am the Don of the Holy Trinity, no man will ever hurt me again.

Now, that's the only thing keeping me above water.

Someday soon, they will all answer to me.

Only me.

Bless me father, for I have sinned.

Everyone that had a hand in hurting me will bleed.

A-fucking-men.

UNDICI

Fuck Off Nicolasi

"Death is the only adventure you have left."
– Captain Hook

Andrea

IT'S BEEN TWO DAYS SINCE BENEDETTO REVEALED TO ME that my father was a twin. Now that I have had time to process this bit of information, I understand why the twins and I share a resemblance. Lorenzo has the same chin dimple as me and Valentino's eyes are the color of honey.

Also just like me.

I still have so many questions and since mom is not here to answer them, I can only count on Benedetto to answer them. Hopefully tonight I'll get more answers than questions.

Roberta informed me that this evening the future leaders of the Holy Trinity will attend the get-together grandfather is hosting in my honor. It was the twins' idea but still Benedetto found it useful to gather everyone and discuss the future of the families. I am honestly tired of this charade. They don't seem to grasp the concept of me not giving one single fuck about their business. I know everything about the Holy Trinity, but I'll have to keep pretending like I'm oblivious to their dealings in the crime world. They can't suspect that I know more than what I'm leading on.

Benedetto still believes my mother didn't tell me about their way of life.

Today I traded in the casual short dress, jean jacket and white sneaker look for a more sophisticated and stylish one. I chose one of my mom's favorite pieces. It's a piece from our winter mother-daughter collection. We worked on it together and it was an experience that helped me realize that I want to follow my mother's footsteps and continue her legacy. My mother made Valentina Co. an international household name and a legendary one at that. Now I want to take it to the next level by creating beauty that breaks boundaries and eliminates stereotypes. I'll take Valentina Co. to the next level once I turn eighteen and I become the sole heir of my mother's legacy.

I look at myself in the mirror, feeling beautiful and sexy. I settled for a tight satin pearl white dress that has a slit up to my left thigh and showcases my long legs. My hair is straightened to perfection and hangs all the way down to my back.

I sit down on the loveseat and add the final touches to this getup, my mom's signature red Louis Vuitton stilettos.

My bathroom door opens and reveals a gorgeous Fallon, with an annoyed look on her stunning face. I detect worry as well.

She is not happy at all with me right now. I led her here under false pretenses. I may have told her it was just the two of us for a movie night. If I would have told her the truth, she would've come up with an excuse to not show up. "I can't believe you are making me interact with these muggles. This friendship is terminated.", she sighs and walks to the door, but just before she grabs the handle, I call out to her.

"Fallon, please do this for me." It's crazy how in so little time, Fallon has become a part of me. I can't go a day without speaking to her. When she's around I feel like I'm not alone in this world, like someone likes the real me and not the fame that comes with my mother's name or the fear that my father's name invokes in others.

Abruptly and without knocking, Valentino opens the door to my room with this crazed look in his eyes while staring at me and it appears, he's trying really hard not to meet Fallon's gaze. *Oh, I am definitely finding out what's going on between them.* "Everyone is waiting for you, you're late." That's all he says before he turns around and makes a move to exit the room.

"Wait, what is it with you and your brother not knocking or waiting for permission to enter a room?" *They really need to stop that, it is annoying.*

He shrugs without a care in the world and leaves the room.

There's something seriously wrong with that dude, he acts like a sociopath. "Do you two know each other?" I ask the question I've been meaning to since their encounter last week.

She's still staring at the spot Valentino was occupying a second ago.

"Earth to Fallon." I wave my hands in her face. – She snaps out of it and looks down at what she's wearing. – "Do you think I should change? Wear something a little bit more presentable?", she asks me.

"Why? A couple of minutes ago you didn't want to be here?" I remind her.

"Yeah, well I changed my mind. I think it will be fun to mess with the Volpe and Parisi brats." – she grins but it doesn't reach her eyes.

"Uhm, sure that's why you want to stay." I laugh.

She flips me off before heading to the walk-in closet to change out of her Captain Marvel pajamas. She's more eager now about this evening than she was thirty minutes ago.

Lucan

I STEP OUT OF MY BRAND-NEW MATTE BLACK MASERATI. It was a gift for my eighteenth birthday courtesy of Tommaso Volpe. There are four cars and a red Ducati parked in the Nicolasi driveway.

"I guess dear brother, as per usual we're the last ones to arrive." My middle sister mutters from the back seat of my car. She's annoyed because our baby sister called shotgun first.

I brought my sisters with me since they are both old enough to know the ins and outs of the Volpe business. The time for the three families to choose the new capo is fast approaching and my sisters have never shied away from this life. We settled this a long time ago; the family believes in women being just as capable as men to run a business and rule the three families, but the girls made it known a long time ago they didn't want to be head of the Volpe family. They have dreams and goals they want to pursue, and trading drugs and guns isn't part of their future plans.

Giana is seventeen and out of the two of us, she's the one that looks and acts most like our mother Natalia Volpe. She has our mother's sun-kissed skin tone, straight dark brown hair, and kind green eyes. She is freakishly smart, strong, compassionate, and would do anything for her family and the people she considers hers. People usually mistake her for a shy and weak girl, just because of her introverted personality but try messing with the ones she holds dear to her heart and I'll guarantee you, she will break every single bone in your body without breaking a sweat. She looks so much like our mother that sometimes it gets too hard to breathe when I'm around her.

She's not her.

She would never betray us.

My sweet Cara, on the other hand, is fifteen going on thirty. She's an old soul that one. If it wasn't for her being my father's replica based only on her looks, I would think she was adopted. My baby sister is the product of an affair between my father and one of his many mistresses. Even though a lot of people in the family look down on my sister because she is the product of adultery, for some unknown reason she is our father's pride and joy. Cara is tall for her age, almost 5'10 with fiery red hair, gray eyes, and a line of adorable freckles across her nose.

I wanted to hate her when my father first brought her home, loving her felt like the ultimate betrayal to my mother, but with just one look at her sweet face, I fell in love. I knew I would do anything to protect her.

Always, just like I would protect Giana.

I could be something more than what my future has in store for me; more than just a fucking common criminal wearing expensive suits. I could've pursued my dream of studying art and one day owning my own studio somewhere far away from this shit place, but there's no one to lead the Volpe family and protect my sisters if I'm gone. So yeah, I stay and do what's expected of me.

For them.

Giana wants to study criminal justice. The irony of her choosing that field when her father and brother are criminals, but I'll always have her back, no matter what path she chooses.

Cara has her head stuck in the clouds and wants to travel the world, model for every expensive high-end brand that she owns and read comic books.

Always so odd my sweet kid sister.

I sometimes worry her heart is too soft for this world and I fear one day this life will break her spirit. I'll do everything in my power to keep them from any harm, if anyone tries to hurt my girls, I'll bleed them dry and bathe in their blood.

"Stay close to me and for all that is holy stay away from the twins, especially Lorenzo." — I make sure they know I mean business. Giana nods and Cara grins. – "I'm talking to you *topina.*", I warn my youngest sister.

She's trouble.

I don't like the way she stares at Enzo, with stars in her eyes and like he hangs the very same stars in her sky, especially when he only has eyes for Giana. That clueless fuck.

What a fucking shit show that will be.

Lorenzo will never put his hands on either of my sisters, I'll cut them off and feed them to that ugly beast he has for a pet before he gets a chance to do so.

The front door opens and the devil himself greets us.

"What took you so long, gorgeous?" It's clear Enzo is talking to Giana. I sense Cara's mood change and I can also see the sadness and disappointment in her eyes.

"Fuck off, Nicolasi, and stay away from my sister." I threaten him and push him out of the way before ushering my sisters inside.

"Come on, Volpe. You know Giana and I are meant to be.", his tone is dripping with sarcasm.

This fucker keeps breaking my baby sister's young heart, without even realizing it.

"Stay the fuck away from them Lorenzo, I fucking mean it." I wait for my sisters to enter the Nicolasi mansion before putting him in a headlock.

"I'm not playing man, at least do it for Cara." He is not blind; he's aware my baby sister has a crush on him. So, why-the-fuck does he taunt her and flirt with Giana right in front of her?

I release him and make my way inside the Nicolasi mansion.

If I would've looked back to where I left him standing, I would have seen the utter devastation in his crazed eyes just by the mention of my fifteen-year-old baby sister's name.

This is going to be a long-ass night.

DODICI

BASTARD

"Oh dear, what an awkward situation."
- Maleficent

Andrea

FALLON AND I WALK DOWN THE LONG STAIRCASE THAT leads to the main room of the mansion. I follow Fallon's gaze while it travels all over the room. The look of awe that takes over her entire face only makes her more endearing to me. She's not a trust fund baby like the rest of us, that is one of the many reasons why I'm so comfortable around her. There's nothing fake or douchey about her.

I glance around the room and notice the butlers and maids located all over the room making sure everything goes smoothly and that the guests are all taken care of.

So extra for just a gathering between a couple of people.

"Damn, bitch! I knew your family was rich, but this place makes Paris's crib look basic as fuck." – Fallon exclaims so loud that Roberta and a few of the staff members stop what they're doing and stare at her in disapproval. Odd enough the younger and less bitter ones try their best to stifle a laugh.

Fallon is anything but subtle.

How did someone as good and genuine as her survive this place for so long without anyone in her corner? What have you've been through Fallon?

She steps away from me and walks to the huge window that has the best view of the gazebo. The look of awe never leaves her face and, in this moment, I admire how truly beautiful and unique Fallon is. When you first meet her, you might overlook her raw beauty because of her unique sense of style and her crazy hairdos. You might not understand her obsession with everything *Marvel* or her weird love for Lord Voldemort. Some might think of her as a weirdo and might take offense of her real- as- fuck and larger than life personality. You might see her as bitchy but all I see is a beautiful soul with lots of opinions that she's never afraid to voice.

She's always beautiful, but today she looks like she stepped out of a high fashion show. Her dark black locks run down her back in perfect waves with some fake green hair extensions we added. I did her makeup following a tutorial of one of Youtube's most influential makeup gurus and I'm quite satisfied with how the look turned out.

She's wearing one of the dresses Benedetto sent for me to try on for the evening, a short, strapless black dress that we paired off with some black combat boots. I offered her one of my Jimmy Choo's, but she told me she wouldn't be caught dead wearing those heels.

She told me she wouldn't feel like herself, so she added some black lipstick and her favorite black widow choker. I find myself smiling while staring at her. I swear Fallon is everything good and fun in the world.

We're both lost in our own heads that we don't even notice the arrival of our guests for the evening. The children of the current mob bosses of Detroit, aka the next generation of criminals.

Both Fallon and I turn and come face to face with three stunning girls, one has a smile on her face while the other two appear like they would rather be anywhere else but here.

The beautiful but very young redheaded girl, with the sweetest smile I've ever seen on a person, approaches us first and in a sweet but high-pitched voice introduces not only herself but the other girls behind her.

"Hi, I'm Cara Volpe. You could say I'm the Iron Man of this gang." She points to the girls behind her and then holds out her hand for me to shake. – "I am so excited to finally meet you! I'm a big fan of your mom, she is one of my top favorite supermodels."

She offers me a sincere smile and there's no malice in her tone when she whispers how sorry she is for my loss. She has no idea how grateful I am that she didn't say it out loud. I don't want anyone's pity, especially not tonight.

Not ever.

"And you are?", the sweet girl is talking to Fallon now.

"I'm Fallon, leader of this two-girl gang. You could say I'm the Batman to her Robin, Sheldon to her Leonard, the..." she's rudely interrupted by one of Cara's sisters. "Yeah, we get it Cara, you found your nerd soulmate. Can we carry on now?" The blonde bombshell with the bitchy attitude says in a bored, almost robotic tone.

"Oh hush, no one's talking to you Arianna." Cara fires back at the blonde stranger that dismissed us and that is now walking to the sitting area without a care in the world. I'm no stranger to catty behavior so if she thought she could intimidate; she is so out of her league.

Cara on the other hand has a sweet and almost gentle vibe, she also seems very mature. The roundness and almost baby like factions of her face shows how young she is. Maybe fifteen? Regardless, she is gorgeous with flaming red hair and big, expressive gray eyes, she could easily fool anyone with how grown up she looks.

I feel eyes on us.

The twins.

Valentino is looking at Fallon with so much disdain that it's almost scary. Lorenzo on the other hand looks like an addict that hasn't had his fix in days. Before I have time to look in the direction, he was looking at just seconds before, his gaze collides with mine and the weirdo smiles at me.

He has the creepiest smile.

It's like smiling pains him and it shows.

He looks demented.

Jesus, I already pity the poor girl that ends up with that nutcase.

Lorenzo is forgotten when I feel goosebumps rise on the back of my neck. I feel him before I see him. *Lucan.*

He's staring at me from across the room with a predatory smile on his handsome face. *Ugh, why does he have to be so attractive?* Tonight, he looks like the future boss of this city, wearing black slacks and a button-down white shirt with the sleeves rolled up and the first two buttons undone. His light brown hair is slicked back, and I can see a tattoo of wings on either side of his neck. At this precise moment he really looks like a vengeful angel. A wicked and very dangerous angel with a sinful grin on his stupid face and an evil twinkle in his eyes.

Yup, Lucifer.

God's favorite but most fucked up angel.

He's coming my way now and I can't stop looking at him. *Ugh, I probably look like one of the botched Barbie's staring at him like he's God's gift to mankind.*

My moment of insanity is over as soon as he opens his mouth. "*Sei bellissima stasera principessa.*" He speaks perfect Italian, of-fucking-course.

Why do these people keep talking to me in Italian? I don't understand half of the shit they say. My mom taught me Spanish because her mother was Puerto Rican. She also wanted me to be bilingual and know more about her culture. My dad wasn't around so I didn't have the chance to learn Italian, although ever since I've arrived, I've picked up some from Benedetto and the maids.

Basically, how to ask for help, for food and to curse at someone. *The basics you know.*

"You should stop referring to me as princess, it is beneath me really." I sass him just because I enjoy the look on his face when I challenge him. He doesn't fall for it and stares at me with an amused look on his face but there's also a challenge behind those blue eyes of his.

He leans in and whispers so only I can hear. "I think what you meant to say is thank you." —We are chest to chest now and I can smell a mix of mint and cigarettes on his breath. — "I did call you beautiful and all", he chuckles so arrogantly that I suppress the urge to slap the stupid grin off his face.

The nerve of this guy.

He called me beautiful, so what? Does he expect me to fall on my knees, or worst on his dick because he complimented my looks?

I'm so lost in my thoughts that I don't notice him reaching

for my face. He's so close that his soft lips gently brush mine. He's not satisfied with the distance between us, so he pulls me closer and wraps both of his arms around me. I don't know why I'm not stopping whatever the hell this is but clearly the smart bitch in me takes a back seat. I make the dumb mistake of meeting him halfway, but he pulls back with the cockiest smile on his annoying face. Lucan turns and looks at everyone in the room that stopped what they were doing and now are witnessing my humiliation.

His laugh is cruel, and he obviously intended for me to look like a fool in front of everyone here.

He set me up.

"Did you actually believe I would kiss you?", he laughs. I swallow my shame and keep my head up. I won't give away how embarrassed I am. How disappointed I am in myself for letting this asshole make an idiot out of me.

"Like I would ever taste the lips of a bastard.", he says with a disgusted look on his face. "Your own father didn't want you, what makes you think I would?"

There it is.

He went for the kill.

I hear gasps behind me and a "Not cool bro" from one of the twins. I'm not sure which one.

Does his immature jab stings? Yes, but I've heard worse, this doesn't faze me.

I don't know what I did to him to be treated this way, but two can play this game.

From my peripheral vision, I see a pretty pissed off Fallon coming towards us. I stick my hand out as a signal for her to stop and let her know that I got this. I offer the room my best smile, the one I only reserve for my enemies.

They will never see me broken or bleeding.

Over my dead-fucking-body.

"I may be the bastard child of Demetrio Nicolasi, but I was the light of Valeria Turner's life. She loved me so hard and so fully that I never doubted her love for me, not for one second. I never felt less than the other kids that did have fathers. She showed me her love every day until the day she died." I tell him with a cruel smile.

"Now, you Lucan, I pity you. Your mother skipped town and never looked back." - I whisper the next sentence so only he can hear. There is no point in hurting his sisters. I bet he did not see that coming. I learnt this bit of valuable information from Fallon. The girl loves gossip just as much as she loves superheroes. I'm thankful for it because the information came in handy tonight.

"She didn't even care to stay long enough to see the man you would grow up to be and I'd rather be a bastard child than an unwanted one." — I chuckle, before leaning back and staring at his furious face once again. — "I win, bitch."

I wink at him, give him my back, and join Fallon where she is now sitting, trying to avoid everyone.

His comment about my dad was uncalled for, but I can be just as cruel, if not more.

"Is something wrong, *bambina*?", a concerned Benedetto asks. — I hadn't even noticed that he had entered the room. His icy stare travels from me to Lucan. I don't know if he can feel the tension in the room but it's hard to miss. Regardless if he does, he chooses not to address the situation.

"No, everything is fine. Just getting to know everyone better." I tell him with a *triumphant smile on my face.*

"Bene, ora andiamo nella sala da pranzo e mangiamo mentre

discutiamo di affari di famiglia." Good, now let's go to the dining area and discuss family business.", he repeats himself in English this time so I can understand.

He stares at me and then at Fallon. He doesn't need to say it out loud because I get what he's trying to say, what needs to be said, Fallon can't know.

Fallon gets the hint and proceeds to leave the room. She heads up the stairs to wait in my room for me. I do not miss Valentino's eyes trailing her all the way up the stairs before she disappears from view.

"Now, follow me." Benedetto says to the room before leading the way to his home office. "It is time for me to step down and for one of you to rise and continue the Holy Trinity's legacy in this city."

I thought living in this place for an entire month would be easy and I could get out unscathed, but maybe I was delusional in thinking it would be that easy. Every day it is becoming clearer that it will be anything but.

Shit.

Now I must endure this evening with people that think of me as public enemy number one and no one in my corner, because the one person that has shown me acceptance is now upstairs waiting for me to be done with this night.

It's getting harder and harder to pretend.

I just want to go home.

TREDICI

FUTURE DON

"Oh, I shall practice my curtsy."
- Scar

Lucan

THE CAPO GATHERS THE NINE OF US IN HIS HOME OFFICE. It is a little crowded, but his face leaves no room for arguments or complaints. This is family business and by the tone of his voice, I'm pretty sure shit's about to get real.

The head of the Holy Trinity of Detroit city sits at his desk and the rest of us stand before him as if we are in some kind of trial, which we actually are. The next generation of Holy Trinity will be chosen soon. The three most ruthless of us all will be the head of each family. I'm the future boss of the Volpe family. The Parisi family will choose between the two oldest sisters since the youngest won't be able to lead…ever.

The Nicolasi family has yet to choose a boss since a new opponent has entered the game. Andrea's arrival has complicated everything.

I wonder if the spoiled brat knows what she has gotten herself into.

The Nicolasi boss was Demetrio but after his death,

Benedetto took over again after decades of not being the Don. He won't make Cassius the Nicolasi boss because he is a traitor, although nobody knows what crime he committed against the family. Cassius is the eldest and he should've been the boss, but something happened there. No one quite knows except the Don, the traitor son and well the other one...but since the dead don't talk, I guess we might never know.

Three Nicolasi children but only one can rule over their family.

Lorenzo, Valentino and now Andrea.

The Parisi family has been run by men for decades now. All of Gabriele Parisi's children were born female, to his utter disappointment. Most Made Men in the families think they are not fit to rule over them but let me tell you something about the two eldest Parisi girls—they are ruthless, they draw you in with their angelic looks and beautiful faces and when you least expect it, they feed on your fears until you bend to their will.

Arianna Parisi is the eldest of the three.

Some men might say she looks like God's favorite angel with her long wavy blond hair with some white streaks in it and deep soulful green eyes, but an angel she is not.

Honestly, there is nothing angelic about that unfeeling bitch.

Arianna is Gabriele Parisi, her father's, most prized possession. *Harsh?* I know. Her father is ready to marry her off to the first willing idiot, little does he know that she has an agenda of her own.

Arianna is no one's trophy wife.

Gabriele's middle child couldn't be more different from her big sister if she tried. Whereas Arianna looks heavenly, Kadra looks like Satan's spawn with her long, straight jet-black hair that she gets from her father and light brown almost yellow eyes that she inherited from her mom.

Kadra has always been strange, even at a young age. Always hiding in the shadows and playing with knives. The black gloves she never takes off are weird as fuck too; she never takes them off not even in the middle of a hot summer day.

She has never been a girl of many words, unlike her sisters.

The Parisi boss doesn't spare her any thought unless it's to keep up with pretenses. No one really knows why he despises her so much, out of all three of his daughters she's the most like him. Kadra is only sixteen years old and could rival any capo in the family. I've witnessed what she can do with just her knife.

We have all grown up together but that doesn't mean we get along. I'm the closest to Lorenzo and Arianna, and Valentino and Kadra formed an unlikely friendship at a young age. I still remember them bonding over who could make a man bleed faster and without getting any of the blood or bodily substances on them.

I scan the room for the youngest Parisi girl, Mila Areya. The sweet but lost girl that reminds me so much of my Cara.

Mila is a mix of her two sisters. She has Arianna's wavy blond hair and Kadra's cat-like yellow eyes. Mila and my two sisters are thick as thieves and I'm kind of relieved that my girls had Mila as a friend, and not the other two psycho sisters.

Just like my Cara is judged within the family, Mila is as well. She was born special, but the Holy Trinity deemed her as damaged goods. The sweet girl was born with a developmental brain disorder, known as Asperger's syndrome. Mila falls somewhere along the autism spectrum. In our eyes, she is perfect but not a lot of people agree. She is awkward in social interactions, sometimes she has issues with communicating with others and she has difficulty interpreting nonverbal communication.

I remember one time I said some sarcastic shit around her, and she just looked at me with a bored and confused look on her face, but she still smiled. She might have trouble understanding other's emotions but, in that moment, she didn't want me to feel bad about my joke and she offered me her beautiful smile.

Cara and Mila are the hearts of our families and we would do anything to keep them from harm.

Our eyes meet and I'm shocked to find no warmth in her gaze. She must know what happened to her sister, shit or it can also be the consequence of growing up in a family that takes away your innocence before the age of fifteen. We are groomed to be ruthless and savages from an early age, we need to be strong and capable to lead not only one family but three. Civilians need to not only follow and respect us but fear us as well.

The time for the next generation of the Holy Trinity to rule over Detroit has come. Our fathers before us went to war with the Nicolasi family and lost every single time. That is why today we have control over a third part of this city but the Nicolasi family still holds more power than the rest of us.

Something that will change the moment they name me the next Don. We all want it but only one of us will reign over Detroit city. My father won't accept failure and won't accept the Volpe family to be second best for far longer. I have my task and I need to fulfill my duty to the family.

The key is fear.

Fear makes even the bravest of men fall in line, bend to our will and fall they will.

And the *principessa* will fall on her knees but only for me.

Andrea

THIS MORNING WHILE I WAS HAVING BREAKFAST ALONE as per usual, Benedetto joined me and turned my world upside down for the second time in the matter of two weeks.

He wants me to lead his family.

A crime family, nevertheless.

What...the...hell.

I know he runs legitimate businesses; they all do but the real money maker is the illegal stuff. The casinos, strip clubs and gun trade. I'm not sure if Benedetto deals with drugs, mom never mentioned if he does but I don't doubt it. The drug trade is where the good money's at. I suspect he deals in many illicit activities outside of Detroit, his reach goes beyond this city.

The other day I was snooping and heard him in his study having a heated conversation with a scary looking older Russian man.

Benedetto addressed the man as Solonik.

Vitali Solonik.

I swear I've heard that name before, but I just can't seem to remember where.

I didn't have time to catch everything they were discussing before one of the maids interrupted my snooping. What I did know is that by the desperate tone in Benedetto's voice, nothing good can come of that allegiance.

It is basic knowledge that Italians and Russian don't get along.

Their argument proved it.

I was wondering why Benedetto was so eager for me to be here, especially since he was absent my entire life.

As the oldest of the three Nicolasi grandchildren he believes it is my duty to be the next boss. I call bullshit, he needs something from me.

He believes I will be Demetrio's successor.

I refuse to be his puppet.

He has two grandsons that were born in this lifestyle and from what I can tell, they both seem to want this. The two psycho twins love the chaos and recklessness of this life, I do not. I do not want to be the boss and I will never be one of them. Once I turn eighteen, I will be out of here.

My thoughts are interrupted by my grandfather's deep and down-to-business voice. "Most of you know the time to choose the next three bosses of each family is fast approaching." — He stares at every single one of us in the eyes. — "Three of you will rule over your own families but only one of you will lead The Holy Trinity and rule over this city."

The Holy Trinity of Detroit city. The three most ruthless and influential crime families in this city, well in the entire country, technically speaking.

Nicolasi.

Volpe.

Parisi.

"*Mio figlio* Deme is no longer with us but in his place, he left his daughter, *mia cara* Andrea." He is staring at me now and as much as he tries to hide his disdain for me behind his devoted grandfather act, it is obvious to see there is no warmth in his eyes.

Only threats.

I can feel the tension rise in the room and although they all probably already knew this; it is abundantly clear that they don't want me here nor do they believe I should be the leader of their shitty crime organization.

I am an intruder in their eyes.

I don't intend to lead shit, only make them sweat a little.

Benedetto has no clue that he just made my time in this place more difficult by the looks of it. I ignore the hateful stares and give my undivided attention to my grandfather. I need to know exactly what I am against and dealing with. These people know a lot more about the Holy Trinity and how they operate. They have lived this criminal life for far longer than I have.

I only came here by force and to maybe find out more about my father. I did not come here to lead a fucking crime family let along three.

I know shit about the criminal world, plus, this is not the life I want for myself. I want to be back home, safe in my mother's world and doing what I love.

My mom's legacy.

I have been keeping track of mom's company and what's going on back in New York since I left a few weeks ago. The media does not know what happened to me and the last time they saw me was at my mother's wake. I'm sure paparazzi took photos of me leaving the chapel with Benedetto and his team of goons, but he went through great lengths to keep them from releasing those photos and statements. I don't even want to know how he managed to do that, but most likely he threatened someone's life, livelihood or he threw his money and status around to get what he wanted.

Lorenzo, the less than smart twin brother, opens his big mouth and shares his two unwanted cents. "I don't think sketching pretty dresses and doing naked photoshoots makes dear Andrea capable of leading three crime families." he snorts. "Get real, grandpa." He laughs at my expense.

"I'm a model not a pornstar, you idiot.", I fire back. The poor dumbass actually believes he could hurt my feelings.

That only makes Lorenzo laugh louder, a genuine laugh.

He is so damn weird.

Benedetto rewards Lorenzo with a furious glare but carries on.

"Now onto more important matters, the Trinity Ceremony is fast approaching, and you need to accomplish the tasks given by the current boss of each family. You will need to do everything that is asked of you and prove yourself worthy. These tasks will push your limits, break your mind and soul." Benedetto stares at each one of us in the eyes. "Man or woman it does not matter, you are equals and as such you will be treated. Only the most ruthless and cunning will reign over this city. It is my time to step down as the boss of all three families and now that Andrea has come home, it is the perfect time for a new leader to be chosen." He turns to me and he has this weird and calculating look on his face.

I swear I don't understand this.

Only one will have the honor of being called the Don and Benedetto wants me to be part of this. *Why? Why me, when he has two grandsons that are clearly more qualified to be made than me?*

The room goes completely silent. From what I learnt they've all grown up together, the three families as one. The ties that bind them together will be broken beyond repaired once they choose between their brothers and sisters for the title of capo.

I scan the room and pay close attention to all of them. Lorenzo is playing with the rings on his fingers with a serious look on his face. I notice how he taps one ring four times before he takes it off and does the same exact thing all over again. I must sound like a broken record by now but there is something seriously wrong with him. He has these weird habits and ticks that no sane person does. On the far-left corner of the room, Valentino is standing looking bored. I don't even think he heard anything Benedetto just said. He seems far away from here.

I look to my right and see the Volpe children standing tall and strong like a united front. Lucan has a smug look on his face, acting like he already has this in the bag, while his sisters are quiet and observing the scene before them. They both are the perfect picture of good Italian girls.

The Volpe family stands united but the Parisi sisters stand like enemies; right next to each other but inches apart. They look ready for combat and not like a united front at all.

Arianna is looking through her phone like she gives two shits about everything that just left Benedetto's mouth. There is something about that girl that's almost scary. How can someone so beautiful and angelic looking and act so frigid and cold, especially towards her sisters.

I learnt the other girls' names; Kadra is the middle sister and Mila the youngest. Kadra has this dark energy all around her, like she is about to explode at any given moment and take us all to hell with her. Unlike her older sister, she doesn't look cold or frigid, she looks angry. I'm not easily scared but the pain and anger behind her cat-like yellow eyes, are a lethal combination. The youngest Parisi is standing far away from her sisters, like she can't bear to be next to them.

Her small hands are shaking; she's nervous. For herself? Her sisters?

Who knows? But one thing I am sure of.

For one to rule, the other must fall.

Benedetto's voice cuts through my thoughts like a double-edged knife.

"Andrea, for the next couple of weeks you will be trained to defend yourself. One on one combat, shooting range, knife, and gun training.", he motions for the silent man that has been here the entire time but was so quiet and undetected that I failed to notice his presence.

Oh, just great.

He won't let this go.

How will I get out of this?

He must've noticed the annoyed look on my face. "I know this is new to you. That is why one of my most trusted men will train you under my supervision." — He points to the man in the corner of the room. — "This is Rian, he will train you in one-on-one combat for the next couple of weeks leading up to the ceremony." — The handsome stranger nods once in my direction and goes back to standing in the shadows.

I sense movement out of the corner of my eyes, so I turn and catch Lucan glaring at Rian while playing with his pocketknife. If looks could kill, my new trainer would be on the other end of Lucan's knife.

And what is his deal?

He is seriously giving me whiplash.

Benedetto dismisses us with one final statement. "Che vinca il migliore uomo o donna.", he gives me one last look before I head out of his office. "In bocca al lupo."

May the best man or woman win.

Good luck.

QUATTORDICI

THE HOLY TRINITY

"Mirror, mirror, on the wall who's the baddest bitch of them all?"
- Unknown

Andrea

IT IS ALMOST MIDNIGHT, AND EVERYONE HAS LEFT EXCEPT the Volpe siblings. The Parisi sisters left soon after grandfather dismissed everyone. Those girls are beautiful, but the two older sisters seem almost robotic. Arianna, the oldest of the three, acts like an unfeeling bitch while the middle one Kadra is too quiet, deadly so. I watched her all night because something about her gave me the heebie jeebies. The blank stare she wore all evening made me anxious-as-fuck.

Nothing or no one impresses her.

The youngest Parisi sister, something about her just tugs at my heartstrings. She seemed lonely. Like she just doesn't belong, trust me I know the feeling.

My thoughts are interrupted by a very pissed off Fallon walking down the stairs towards us. The green *Slytherin* pajamas she is wearing and the slippers of the elf from that wizard movie she loves so much, makes her look more adorable than threatening. She was reluctant to come down, but I needed her as a backup in case shit went down with Lucan again.

"So, Drea, it must be difficult getting used to the calm and quiet of this city compared to how crowded and noisy New York is." —Giana, the middle child of the Volpe family breaks the uncomfortable silence first.

Unlike her bubbly younger sister, Giana seems a little standoff-ish and shy. She's beautiful though, with light brown hair that stops just above her shoulders and the same baby blues as her older brother. I notice the younger sister, Cara, does not share the same skin tone or any of the same characteristics as her older siblings.

"It was at first." I answer truthfully. Detroit is not so different from New York. It's not a horrible place but it's just not home. I also detest most of the kids at Holy Trinity Academy because they act superior and their holier-than-thou personalities irritates me to no end. I have nothing good to say about that place or those people and my mom always taught me to shut my trap if I have nothing nice to say. Unless someone messes with me, then it's fair game.

Besides, everyone is the same here.

The popular kids are not welcoming to others and they just keep to themselves, for fuck sakes even the nerds act like bitches.

They act like everyone else is beneath them.

I also hate how judgmental the older generation is. The first-time grandfather introduced me to some of his acquaintances, I was not oblivious to their disapproving stares and I'm sure when they got home, I was the topic of their conversations.

I dislike how I'm always surrounded by non-stop silence. In this house, nobody is ever here besides the maids and guards, but they pay me no mind. Benedetto is always gone; God only knows where Cassius is most of the time and the twins? Well, they act as if I don't exist.

At night I can't escape the silence, thoughts of what could've been plague me until the point it's hard to breathe.

At night is when I miss her the most.

When I dream of only her and my life back in New York.

It's almost sad how I made mom my everything. It was just us against the world and now I'm alone here surrounded by hungry wolves.

They can never know that I feel everything, sometimes too damn much.

That's my only weakness now that mom is gone.

My vulnerable heart.

So, I suck it up and offer them my best smile, the fake one.

The one I perfected the day after my mother died and I had to face the world and chaos she left behind

"I do miss New York and my friends, but I talk to them almost all the time and I keep tabs on my mother's businesses through my uncle Emilio." I ignore Lorenzo's petty snort and carry on. "This city is...well unusual but after years of so much noise and a hectic lifestyle, I appreciate the chill environment."

I am thankful for Fallon's interruption when she asks about what went down at the meeting with Benedetto.

"I believe that's none of your business, witch." Valentino speaks after being silent and merely observing all night. I'm surprised he's even acknowledging her, since every time they're in the same vicinity he acts like she doesn't exist.

"And I believe I was not asking you, dickhead but thanks for the compliment by the way." She smiles sweetly and flips him off before asking again, but this time Giana answers her.

"Valentino is right, what was said is family business, only family or associates are allowed to know. — Giana smiles kindly at me. — "Although, it wouldn't kill you to be nicer, Val."

"Being nice to the bitch is what fucked me up, so yeah it actually can." Valentino stands and leaves the room after that nasty remark towards Fallon.

What the actual fuck is going on here? I have only known Fallon a couple of weeks and yes, maybe it is too early to feel so protective of someone you just met but I can't help it. It is like I have been waiting for her all my life. She feels like someone I can trust, especially now that I need someone in my corner.

"I'll just meet you upstairs, Drea.", she clears her throat, a nervous habit I've noticed she has. "I'm tired.", she murmurs so quietly that I almost miss it.

I wish I had.

There is so much pain behind those gorgeous dark eyes of hers and I wish I could erase it and ease her pain.

"You don't want to know, trust me." — Cara has also been quiet until now. — "Fallon and Val are complicated." This sweet girl is a whole ass grown adult in a fifteen-year-old body.

"I'm bored, let's go." Lucan rises from his seat and heads to the door but stops to wait for his sisters to follow.

Both girls stand but before they leave, they have one last thing to say.

"I'm glad you're here." — Giana surprises me. — "You should know that it wasn't always like this, this was a man's world before the Parisi sisters changed it all just by being born and changing the rules. They proved themselves to be just as ruthless and cunning as any man. Their father's men follow them, but our families need a little bit more convincing.", she lowers her voice. "If you want to survive you need to make sure you don't reveal any weakness. You don't ever back down and show fear. Even if you are losing, if you can't breathe, if it's too much, you don't tap out." She touches my hand in a supportive and kind gesture before she turns and follows her siblings to the door before they all leave.

Lorenzo stands from the love seat that he was sitting on just a couple of minutes ago and walks towards me. I'm still staring at the door when he begins to speak.

"You know cousin, you are out of your depth here. To become a full member of the Cosa Nostra and a "man or woman of honor" we must take part in an initiation ceremony. The ceremony involves a significant ritual, oaths, blood, and an agreement is made to follow the rules of the Holy Trinity," he explains. He proceeds to tell me how the ceremony will be held after every single one of us completes our task given to us by the current boss of our respective families.

"What happens if someone refuses to go along with the chosen task?" I am curious because there's no way in hell I will be a part of this.

"It's quite simple dear Andrea." – a cruel smile appears on his face as he answers me. — "If you don't go through with your task it will be considered an act of rebellion and a betrayal to the three families and trust me when I say this: you will wish you would've man up and done your job, because there is no escaping us." His tone unnerves me. I catch a glimpse of hurt in his eyes before it's gone. Like it was just a figment of my imagination.

I remember Benedetto mentioning the blood oath. The last step before you become a full member of the Holy Trinity and a Made Man or Woman.

"Grandfather mentioned a blood oath, what is that all about?"

The freak smiles at the mention of blood.

"It is a frequently broken rule, but also punishable by death." he leaves my side and walks to the stairs. "Basically, if you turn rat, you die." With those parting words, he disappears.

As morbid as it is, I'm not afraid to die. I'm more afraid of living a life I don't want. To end up in this hell hole and become one of them.

Staying in Detroit and being part of The Holy Trinity means leaving all my dreams behind.

A buzzing noise coming from the main entrance interrupts my sad-as-fuck train of thought. *Who could it be at this hour?* Everyone left.

I do not wait for the maid to open the door, I do it myself.

Ugh, I should have waited for the maid to answer the door, now I must deal with him.

I am seconds away from closing the door in his face when he forcefully grabs my neck and shoves me back into the house. I try to fight him off, but he is so much stronger than me. Lucan maneuvers us until my back is to his front.

From this position, I can feel his growing erection. "If you ever mention my mother again sweetheart, I will rip your heart out of your chest and give it to your grandfather on a silver fucking platter.", he threatens.

I break free from his grasp until we are face to face. "Same goes for you baby, next time you mention either of my parents, I'll cut off your dick and I'll shove it down your throat." I smack his cheek lightly and leave him standing there.

I'm almost to the second floor of the mansion when he laughs maniacally.

Fucking psycho.

"You have no idea what you just started, principessa." he rubs his hands over his lips, smearing my red lipstick all over his mouth while offering me a sick grin. "I'll make you regret that,", he promises.

"And I'll make you regret the moment you thought you were any match for me."

Feels good to have the last word.

Take that asshole.

Lucan

FUCK, I'M HARD.

The little bitch has consumed my every thought since the moment her sexy ass arrived in my city.

Tonight, she proved she can hold her own against me.

The threats coming out of those sinful, plump, red lips made me hard, so much so that I need to get fucked before I lose it.

I haven't gotten hard over a girl running her mouth since I was a twelve-year-old horny kid.

I underestimated Andrea. That's a mistake I won't ever repeat.

She stands in the way of me being boss, they all do. I'll kill anyone that threatens both my sister's safety.

When it comes to Andrea, I won't think twice before I spill her blood and watch the substance — the same color as her cherry red lips — drip from my favorite knife.

I might fuck her while doing so.

I've always been good at multitasking.

QUINDICI

Rian

"Playtime is over kids."
- Gaston

Andrea

I HAD A ROUGH NIGHT LAST NIGHT, EVERYTHING THAT was said in the meeting plagued my thoughts and then the fucking nightmares wouldn't leave me alone. Not even Fallon's company could keep the nightmares at bay.

She slept like a baby while I've been up since 2:00 am, losing myself in my sketchbook. The only good thing about the miserable and sleepless night is that I came up with some beautiful designs for the company. I need to be prepared to prove to the board members that I am more than qualified to run my mother's business affairs and that there's no better option than me. If they find any reason for me not to take my mother's place as CEO, they'll appoint someone else and that's just not an option.

It is not only my dream but my duty.

I promised her.

But sadly, I don't own all the shares of Valentina Co., and they have more votes than I do. They can easily overturn any decision I make, so I need to play nice with them to get what I want.

A small amount of the shares belong to an unknown investor. Since mom passed away, I've been trying to locate this silent investor, but it has been almost impossible to track him down. *What the hell was mom thinking adding a silent investor? It's* not like she needed the money.

I swear, sometimes it feels like I never fully knew my mom.

She held so many secrets so close to her heart that it was almost impossible to reach them.

I press send to the email and wait till it goes through before I slip my phone back into the pocket of my sweatpants. The head of the designing team at Valentina Co, has been hounding me nonstop for some new ideas for the next spring collection. Last night I came up with some great looks for every body type and for all kinds of women. I didn't lie when I said I wanted to help break stereotypes, everyone should be represented in the fashion industry. It is high time the fashion world broke out of the discriminatory and judgmental mentality.

I want to expand to men's clothing as well.

I walk out to the patio and find my new trainer leaning against a lounge chair smoking a cigarette. He has a sour look on his face. He doesn't hide the fact that he is displeased with my tardiness.

Today, I have my first training session with Benedetto's very own personal bodyguard, Rian.

In the meeting last night, I didn't really pay enough attention to the silent man whose job is to protect the current capo of the Nicolasi family with his life.

Rian is attractive, that I did notice but what caught my attention first is the number of tattoos that cover his body. Every man that works for Benedetto has the clean-cut, respectable Made

Men man look while Rian looks like a common street criminal, a dangerous and reckless one at that.

"You're late." He puffs a smoke ring my way before he puts the cigarette out and throws it at my feet.

"First off, how fucking rude." I bend down, pick the cancer stick from the grass and walk to the nearest trash can to dispose of it." I make my way back to where he is standing now. He assesses me with a calculating but yet amused look on his face.

"And also, dude you have to give me some credit for the simple fact I made it out here in the first place. Who the hell wants to train at 6:00 am in the morning on a fucking Saturday? Not me that's for sure."

After everyone left last night, Fallon and I stayed up late watching reruns of some nineties sitcom that she loves. She was acting weird the entire time and I bet it had everything to do with a certain silent and broody twin. Valentino really is an asshole, and he doesn't even try. It just comes naturally to him.

I also noticed that she was hiding bruises on her neck with foundation. She did a really good job applying the perfect amount of makeup to cover the bruises so no one would be able to see what she is hiding underneath it.

I did notice though.

I asked what happened and she just shrugged it off like it was normal and said: "Just a normal day in the James household." — *How can anyone hurt Fallon?*

For the past couple of weeks, I've been hanging around her. She avoids all topics about her family. She has never invited me into her home and all the times we have hung out together, it has been on my turf. I must find a subtle way to ask her what is going on. We all have demons, but she doesn't have to face them alone.

Not anymore.

Once I'm free to get out of this place, I'm hoping she'll follow once she graduates. She shared her dreams and goals with me. Fallon wants to study photography in New York. I can also hook her up with some acquaintances of my mom, maybe they can offer her an internship or something.

I completely forgot about the asshole standing before me until he snaps his tattooed fingers in my face. "Hey, kid, snap the fuck out of it and let's do this. I have shit to do." How did I not notice his accent before?

Very hot and very Irish.

How the hell did an Irish guy find his way into the Italian mafia?

Ugh, who the hell cares? Honestly, it is too early for this shit.

I find it extremely difficult, not to mention painful, to hold back the sarcastic remark threatening to slip free from my lips.

"Yeah, yeah whatever. Let's get this over with." I follow him to the patio table where he has every torture item imaginable including grenades.

Why would he need a fucking grenade?

He notices my dumbfounded look and takes advantage of it.

"Have you ever held a gun kid?", he mocks.

He really is an ass.

"Never needed to before, so no." I am honest. This shit is new to me, but as the daughter of a famous supermodel I had bodyguards working around the clock.

"Here." He throws a gun at me.

A fucking loaded gun.

Thankfully, I catch it before it hits the ground and goes off. I grab the gun with shaking fingers and hold it as far away from me as I possibly can. It would be a tragedy if I shoot an eye out.

Still, I'm furious.

"What the hell!" I yell. "It could've gone off." I hand him back the damn gun.

I did not sign up for this shit.

"Please kid, like I would hand you a loaded gun. I care about my life." he turns around and leads the way to the shooting range behind the pool house.

The Nicolasi mansion has everything you could ever need.

I reluctantly follow him all the while shooting daggers at his back

Ugh, how the hell did I get myself into this mess?

Fucking Benedetto, that's how.

"What are you waiting for, princess? I don't have all fucking day.", he says that at the same damn moment a gun goes off.

He shot at me.

The asshole shot at me because I took my time catching up to him.

What in the ever-loving hell...?

Not only have I been threatened, mocked, and ridiculed since I have arrived in this city but now, I can add being shot at by an Irish psycho.

I can't wait to be done with this damn place.

SEDICI

The Jerk Has Manners

"Morality isn't black and white."
– Cruella De Vil

Andrea

IT'S THE MONDAY AFTER THE GATHERING AND FALLON still won't open up about what kind of nightmares she's facing at home. She shrugged it all off like it was normal to walk around hiding bruises – real painful looking ones on her neck might I add–with makeup foundation. She also refuses to talk about Valentino or their tumultuous past. Every time I tried to ask or bring him up in conversation, she shut me down. Fallon wouldn't budge so I just dropped it and let her keep her secrets for now. Some things are better left in the past, but her current situation at home concerns me and what kind of friend or even human being would I be if I just stand by and watch the sweetest of souls get abused in any way.

Nope.

I'm taking her with me, once I leave this place in a couple of weeks.

My mind has been occupied all weekend with Fallon's problems and concentrating on healing my body after that crazy

Irish abused it in our "training session". It felt more like a beating up Andrea for fun kind of session. Every time he got a hit in, the freak smiled and sometimes even laughed. *Remember when I said he was quiet and observing?* Fuck no. He's the same kind of psycho breed as Lucan and his evil twin sidekicks.

I'm still reeling after mine and Lucan's encounter the other night. I keep beating myself up for falling for his shit and not seeing through his mind games. *How could I have let him pull one over me?* It was a lapse in judgment, and it won't happen again.

It can't.

I finish applying my makeup and look at my reflection in the mirror. My blonde hair is straightened to perfection without a hair out of place, I successfully mastered the wing eye technique and I'm quite proud of myself. Nikki makes it seem so easy on her tutorials and trust me it is anything but. My plump lips are painted a deep shade of red but that's all. I don't wear a lot of makeup, mom used to warn me that if I used too much makeup in my youth, I would accelerate the process of aging. The thought of looking like Dobby, the house elf, in my twenties scared the crap out of me so much so that I kept my makeup to a bare minimum.

I am almost done zipping up my boots when I hear a loud engine come up the driveway. I leave my spot on the bed and walk to the window to see who has arrived at the mansion this early in the morning.

There's a black Maserati with black tinted windows parked in the driveway, it looks expensive and extra as fuck.

Must be a friend of the twins.

The driver steps out of the car and I know my day just went to shit.

Why must God keep testing my patience?

It's Satan himself and I'm ashamed of myself for admitting that he looks good, smoking hot actually. His hair is styled as usual, with ray bans on and his tie loose like he gives no fucks if he gets called out for breaking the academy's dressing code.

He walks around his car until he's standing just below my balcony.

There's a pull between us and I know he feels it too. I know this because he wouldn't act like a wild animal that feels threatened when I get too close every time I'm around. I could use it to my advantage, and I will if he keeps interfering in my life.

I shouldn't feel anything but animosity and aversion towards him but, if I'm honest with myself, I feel intrigued by him. It makes me sick and makes me question my sanity because this guy's whole mission since we met is to humiliate me, remind me that I don't belong here and send me back to "my world".

I'll go back to my world once I have figured out what secret mom was hiding on her last days on earth. And, on the day of my eighteen birthday, I am out of here.

My dad.

I shouldn't care about him since he left and didn't care enough about me to stay.

Now that I am an orphan, I find myself wondering why. *Why did he leave us? Was his life in any danger here? Did something happen that kept him away?*

Those questions keep running through my mind and I just can't move on and build a future for myself when all these ghosts won't let me be.

I hope I find answers before I leave this city and everyone in it behind. I can't let Lucan step in and ruin everything I ever wanted.

There's so much to lose.

Shit, I am surrounded by wolves everywhere.

For a second there I forgot my current situation.

The devil is here.

I open the balcony door and walk to the railing. Lucan is patiently waiting and motions for me to come down.

And they say chivalry is dead.

"Why are you here, Lucan?" Dealing with his weird mood swings is exhausting and it is not something I want to do this early in the morning.

"Come down *principessa*, you are riding to school with me from now on." He smiles that incredibly sexy and extremely annoying smile of his.

"Yeah, no, I don't think so. Get lost." I turn my back on him and close the balcony's door behind me. I disconnect my phone off its charger, grab my bag and head downstairs to find someone to take me to the academy.

I'm at the top of the stairs when the doorbell rings and I know exactly who is behind that door.

Can't he take a hint?

I can't be the only girl that has ever rejected this guy.

What is his damage?

I stay rooted in place as one of the younger maids, Layla, answers the front door and greets Lucan. From my spot at the top of the stairs, I can't make out what they're saying. By the looks of her reddened cheeks and how she is playing with a lock of her hair, the asshole is charming the ugly skirt off her.

I clear my throat loudly to announce my presence. I'm saving sweet Layla from further embarrassment. She should thank me.

"Look who came to take you to school Andrea.", she offers me a sickly-sweet smile, unaware of the evil bastard that she just let in the house. "Lucan offered to drive you to the academy since you don't have many friends, dear."

Oh, so the bitch is not so sweet after all.

I swear, I feel the spirit of the Holy Ghost restraining the catty bitch inside me before I snap.

I breathe through my nose a couple of times before I respond to her snarky comment. "Oh, isn't that a lovely idea," — I smile sweetly at them— "but I don't think so. I prefer if one of Benedetto's drivers takes me to the academy."

Layla shakes her head while Lucan stares at me with annoyance written all over his stupid face. "Your grandfather strictly told us that from now on you will ride to and from school with Mr. Volpe." I don't miss the warning in her tone and the way her eyes soften when she mentions Lucan's name.

Crap, since I don't have a car and none of Benedetto's men will take me, I guess I'll have to suck it up and accept his offer.

Layla is not done though. "Also, Lucan here made an excellent point."

"And what point might that be?" I find it almost impossible not to roll my eyes at how ridiculous this entire situation is. *How come no one seems to see through his good boy act?*

"That you are new to the academy and may need someone to have your back, and Mr. Nicolasi agreed. So, go on or you'll be late."

He smirks triumphantly at me and it just enrages me more. I want to smack that obnoxious smile right off his face.

I need to pick my battles with this one, so I give in and reluctantly follow him to his car. It is obvious that he's very pleased with himself at this moment.

We reach the passenger door of his Maserati, he opens it for me and what do you know, the jerk has manners.

"Get the fuck in *principessa*, we don't have all day." He snaps at me.

And just like that he opens that big mouth of his and ruins it.

DICIASSETTE

Do You Want Me Principessa?

"He's a guy."
- Hades

Lucan

WHAT THE FUCK AM I DOING?

When it comes to Andrea Nicolasi, my good judgment goes to hell. I'm supposed to make this girl hate me enough to leave town and go back to wherever the hell she came from. I even went as far as humiliating her in front of everyone but still, she won't break.

The little principessa is tough as nails and not a pushover like I initially thought.

So, what makes a girl like her break?

Her mom is dead. She has no one besides a family that could care less about her and a loner for a friend.

From what I've observed in her short stay in this city, she has grown close to Fallon. Maybe if I threaten her little friend it might do some damage, but Fallon is tougher than she looks.

The only one that can do some serious damage is Valentino.

And he will.

It's just a matter of time.

Andrea cares too much even when she pretends that she doesn't and that will be her downfall. *Doesn't she know that letting people in only causes heartache and opens the door to betrayals?*

I turn and study her face. — She's nervous, that I can tell. She is clutching that necklace of hers like it might protect her from me.

Silly little princess, don't you know by now that no one can protect you from me?

Andrea keeps looking out the window in the passenger seat and has not said one word since we left the Nicolasi mansion. The stubborn brat refuses to acknowledge my presence and it's starting to piss me off.

We are ten minutes away from the academy when she decides to talk. "So, what's your endgame?", she asks with a hostile tone.

"What do you mean?" The cunning little vixen is so suspicious.

The girl is smart, she shouldn't trust me.

Or any of us for that matter.

"Oh, don't play games, Lucan." —she's staring at me now — "You don't seem like the type of guy that does something nice for someone else and not expect something in return. "So, I'm asking you again, what do you get out of spending time with me on these car rides to school?"

Even in the car, I tower over her and this gives me the perfect angle to look down her shirt. The first two bottoms of her shirt are undone, and I can see the straps of her red bra.

I may not like her bratty attitude, but my dick does and a whole lot.

Fuck.

I adjust myself without her noticing because I sure as fuck don't want her knowing I have a hard-on for her, but she does notice and by the triumphant look on her face, she's enjoying it.

Huh, the principessa wants to play?

Then let's play.

When we reach a red stop light in the middle of traffic, I turn the engine off.

"What the hell!" she screams. "What are you doing, you idiot! There are people behind us." She is so loud that I think she fucked up my eardrums.

I turn in my seat to face her. "Do you want me, principessa?"

"No, I do not, you creep! — What's wrong with you? Turn the engine back on and keep driving.", she screams at me.

Oh, how I would love to hear her scream for me.

"Lucan, come on, you could cause an accident." She's nervous now.

Good.

She should be.

"I'll turn the car back on when you answer my question."— It started as a joke but now I really want to know. — "I won't ask again." I warn her.

"Oh yeah, and what are you going to do if I don't answer your question?" she mocks.

In one quick move, I grab her face and shut her the hell up with my mouth.

She's rigid.

I'm sure she didn't see that coming. I'm about to pull away from her sinful lips before I become obsessed with them when she grabs me by the tie and kisses me back.

Fuck, her sweet tongue will be the death of me.

After a moment of ravishing each other's mouths, we pull apart and stare at one another. I'm trying to calm down my racing pulse when the little temptress runs her tongue all over her bottom lip before biting it. I zero in on her tongue and I'm caught off guard when she pushes me away from her and I land back on the driver's seat.

She just beat me at my own game.

The fuck.

Thankfully, she's the one that breaks the silence first.

"Not as much as you want me." she winks and goes back to staring at the road ahead of us waiting patiently for me to drive us the hell out of there.

I ignore her comment because I'm lost for words.

She one upped me.

So, I turn the engine back on and head to the academy before I do something, we both might regret later.

Andrea: 1

Lucan: 0

Shit.

DICIOTTO

FALLON & VAL

"If two people are meant to be together, eventually they'll find their way back."
– Chuck Bass

Fallon

Dreaming of someone you know you can't have,
Missing them every hour of every damn day,
And knowing that their hearts will never be fully yours.
It's the worst fucking feeling in the world,
Cause all you can do is dream,
All you have is dreams of them.

THE ROOM IS SILENT EXCEPT FOR MR. GONZALEZ'S WORDS of encouragement towards my poem and Drea's clapping. I look around the classroom and everyone has a bored expression on their faces, turds.

They have no taste whatsoever.

"Ms. James, I didn't know you had a poet's soul. Your words are tragically beautiful, and I think we can all agree. Job well done!", he praises me. "Now, who's next?", he asks the class.

I take my seat right next to Andrea and find her smiling proudly at me.

"Why are you smiling at me like that?", She can't be that daft to think I wrote this poem, right? Well, it was an Oscar worthy performance if you ask me.

"Dude, you were amazing!" she whisper-yells. "Why didn't you tell me you were so good at writing poetry?"

"Girl, I am not that deep, but someone on Pinterest is." I wink and laugh at the incredulous look on her face.

"Fallon, you did not." She says laughing while shaking her head at me. The teacher is about to call on someone when the classroom door opens and the Grim Reaper himself walks in, interrupting Mr. Gonzalez's mid-sentence.

After all this time he is still the star of all my dreams and fantasies. Two years and still he owns a part of me, the part of me that believed every lie and every promise that Valentino made me.

Since the day I started Holy Trinity, two years ago, I noticed everything about him.

Val wears black clothing, usually, turtlenecks, that make him look older and wiser than his seventeen years — mysterious too. The twins are a year younger than me, but Val skipped a grade whereas his twin brother did not.

Lorenzo is not book smart like his twin, so he stayed behind.

I knew everything about him — he was everything to me — but he ruined it.

He ruined us.

I exposed the most vulnerable parts of myself to him and he mocked me. I showed him my scars, in hope that he would heal them but all he managed to do was leave me with more.

He warned me he would ruin me and, still, I wrapped my arms around his demons, but he only used me to quiet them until I wasn't useful anymore.

Valentino and I? We were toxic from the start, but somehow, he managed to decimate all my carefully build walls and steal my very weak and broken heart only to stomp on it and throw it away like it never meant anything.

"She's just like every other hoe in this city. So ready to spread her legs for a Nicolasi." Their cruel laughs still haunt me. *"The only reason I gave her the time of day was because it was asked of me."*

I will never forget or forgive his betrayal.

We both lost everything that day, all because he lied.

"Mr. Nicolasi, what a surprise to see you in my class. What can I do for you?" Val approaches our teacher's desk and hands him a pink piece of paper, then proceeds to walk by me and choose a seat at the back of the class, next to Lucan's now empty one.

I make the stupid mistake of looking over my shoulder to where he's sitting and catch his hateful stare.

He hates me.

Right back at you baby.

DICIANNOVE

Confusing As Fuck

"But mostly, I hate the way I don't hate you, not even close, not even a little bit, not even at all."
– Kat Stratford

Andrea

I'M PISSED.

How did I let Lucan get to me again?

Now he knows that a tiny, stupid part of me finds him somewhat desirable. After the kiss, we drove to the academy in complete silence. *What was there to say really?*

I could tell that I surprised him with my reaction to his stupid stunt in the car.

I surprise my damn self.

Don't get me wrong it was a mind-blowing and panty-dropping kiss, but I won't have him thinking that he has me in the bag or has the upper hand.

He certainly does not.

He confuses me. One day he threatens me in front of everyone, humiliates me by calling me a bastard, then he defends me against Cassia's vicious words and now he kisses the life out of me.

I've never been boy crazy, never acted like all the other girls that kiss the ground their bullies walk on. I was never that girl and I don't intend to start now. Those type of girls gives me secondhand embarrassment, not because they are comfortable with their sexuality and know exactly what they want; my problem is with the ones that let men walk all over them and let themselves be treated like they're disposable.

Let's practice self-respect ladies, it is free after all.

Besides I'm just a game to him, he made that abundantly clear time and time again with every joke and derogatory word towards me. I need to stay focused on my goal and not get sidetracked by a pretty face with an ugly soul. One day he hates me, and the next he wants me.

His mixed signals are so confusing.

After we reached the school grounds, he walked me to my first class without saying a single word to me. Everyone kept staring at us as we walked the halls of Holy T. Some girls looked green with envy and others were just throwing curious glances our way.

Everyone must be wondering why their "king" is walking a peasant, by their standards, to class. In this place, it doesn't matter that my mother was a world- renowned supermodel, that I carry the Nicolasi name and that my grandfather practically owns this city. Lucan made it clear that I was not welcome here and apparently, in this academy, his word is law.

He usually sits next to me during Lit class, but he didn't come in with me today. He just walked me to the door and then left. *—Where did he go? And why do I even care?*

Ugh, this is what happens when you let the devil in.

My annoying thoughts about the whereabouts of a certain blonde asshole are interrupted by my cousin Valentino. He walks towards us and takes the seat right behind Fallon.

For someone that claims to loathe the very existence of Fallon, he sure loves to be near her

I know he chose that seat because of her. There are at least six empty chairs and he chose the one behind her.

Fallon & Val — who would've thought? My girl is loud, sarcastic, funny and I say this with all the love in the world. She's kind of a gigantic nerd. She stays at home on Friday nights and watches reruns of The Big Bang Theory with her cat, a cat she named Eyre. She also loves reading the classics, books that basically no one our age reads.

Oh, did I mention she owns a pet snake? I shiver just at the thought of that ugly ass thing she calls Petunia.

Gross.

She's perfect, but not everyone sees her as I do.

On the other hand, Valentino is the silent type. He wears only black and his wardrobe consists of high-end brands only. He's the quarterback of the football team but I never see him with the jocks. He's always by himself or with Lucan and his twin brother Lorenzo.

What I did notice is that he always carries a journal and a pen with him. I'm curious about that, maybe one day I'll care enough to ask him about it.

I look at Fallon sitting beside me and she's so stiff that she looks like she's not breathing. Valentino joining this class triggered her. I wish I could do something to take that look away from her pretty eyes. I recognize that emotion staring back at me every time I look at my reflection.

It's grief.

Mr. Gonzalez has been calling on us one by one to go up to

the front of the class and recite our poems. One of the botched Barbie look alike is next.

"My beauty is rare and so is my hair,
When I enter a room everyone stares,
I'm one of a kind,
No one compares...

This girl cannot be serious. I tune her out before I lose a brain cell listening to her so-called poem. Once she's done, she takes the empty seat next to Valentino.

Seriously, these girls are like the plague.

"Hey baby, I've missed you." — Valentino is now writing in his journal and is paying no attention to her. — "Are we still on for tonight?", she purrs before grabbing his bicep and turning him towards her, so she has better access to his mouth.

I look away from them before I throw up my breakfast and find Fallon concentrating very hard on the board in front of her, with a murderous frown on her face.

Shit.

VENTI

The Principessa Can Save Her Fucking Self

"You don't know what you're capable of until you have to do it."
– June Osborne

Lucan

THAT KISS.

That fucking kiss.

Why can't I get it out of my head? I've kissed plenty of bitches before, but there's something about her that feels... right.

Andrea.

My enemy and a threat standing in the way of me keeping my world safe. The girl with so much sorrow in her eyes and so much fire in her heart. As much as I try to remember that she's my task, I still can't get her out of my system and that's fucking dangerous.

She's the sweetest poison and I wouldn't mind drowning in her.

If I allow myself to own her— mind, body, and soul. There's no going back. I'll lose myself in her.

I received my task — her. Tommaso made it clear that I was to get rid of Demetrio's kid. The family made it known that they won't accept a bastard that knows nothing about our dealings to lead them. Benedetto knows this and still, he's pushing Andrea on all of us.

For me to become the capo of the three founding families...I must make sure Andrea Nicolasi goes back to New York for good.

Just the thought of her being five hundred and eighty-five miles away, doesn't sit right with me.

Ring, ring, ring...

I pick up my phone from my nightstand and I'm surprised by the caller. It's midnight, this is unusual for her. I pick up on the fourth ring. "What's wrong?", her future is being dictated by men and she might go rogue.

"We need to talk, come down." That's all she says before ending the call.

Something is definitely wrong.

I leave my bed, walk to my window and there she is. She ditched her bodyguard, again. She has a bad habit of doing that and one day she will find herself in a fucked-up situation with no one to save her.

I leave my room and head to my family's garden where Arianna is waiting for me. I find her sitting under the gazebo, staring up at the stars with a worry expression on her face.

I've known Arianna since we were kids. She never shows emotion, I don't even think she has any. Some call her an ice princess because of her cold exterior and sometimes bitch personality, but today that's not the case.

I've never seen her this way before.

She looks almost broken.

"Did I ever tell you the story behind my middle name?", she says while still looking at the night sky. I don't bother answering her question since I'm sure she doesn't care what I have to say. She just needs someone who will listen to her.

We have a full moon tonight and it's could as fuck. Still, I stay because this is a welcome distraction.

There's something melancholic and almost sad about this night.

"My grandmother used to tell us tales about her own grandmother, Antonietta Parisi, and how she was a dreamer that lived in a poor village back in Italy. She had dreams of coming to America and making a life for herself, where everyone had equal opportunity to succeed and women were treated just as the men were. Her papa had other plans for her. He was a greedy man and a selfish father, so much so that he sold his only daughter to the highest bidder. To a criminal, Giorgio Parisi, who turned out to be a sick and sadistic bastard that raped and abused her and even went as far as to make money off her body by selling her. She was his possession, so no one dared to question him. Years and years of abuse hardened her soft heart to the point that she turned cold and lost touch with reality. Her heart wasn't filled with childlike dreams and hopes any longer. It was just a useless organ beating in her chest."

Her voice trembles and her body is shivering.

What's the point of this story? I'm freezing my balls off.

"One cold December night, she gave birth to fraternal twins, a boy and a baby girl. They were the product of her pain and abuse. She named the little girl Luna. *Do you know what happened to sweet baby girl Luna?* – Giorgio, satisfied with his male heir, found no use for the baby girl, so he suffocated her and left her in the middle of the woods. If the lack of air didn't kill her then the wolves certainly did. Filled with despair, Antonietta followed him to where he had run off to with their infant daughter, but she was too late. He murdered the baby."

"They silently walked back to their cabin and she waited for him to fall asleep and in a fit of rage, she lost it and killed her husband that very same night right before hanging herself off a tree. The baby boy was found later by Giorgio's brother and he and his wife raised him as their own. No one ever found the body of baby girl Luna and boy grew up to be just like his father and so did the next generation after him."

Arianna's voice shakes with anger now. Long gone is the sadness that surrounded her just a couple of minutes ago.

"The Parisi men only conceived male babies, until I was born. So, my mother named me after the lost Luna, she was the last Parisi female until us."

Shit, imagine being named after a girl that was murdered by her father and then was eaten by wolves. Yeah, the story is tragic but come on Arianna's mom has always been a cold bitch and this only proves it.

"Just like baby Luna, I too was born on a cold December night under a full moon. – Did you know full moons have been associated with odd insane behavior including suicide, fits of violence and illegal activities? Some also say that children born on full moons are born cold and heartless because the Roman, goddess of the moon, Luna, would ride her silver chariot across the dead sky and steal the babies' souls."

She is laughing now; the sound is strange coming from her lips. Arianna never laughs.

"Every time mama was angry with me; she would tell the story of how when I was born, I didn't make a sound and my frail skin was so cold. She believes the moon goddess must've stolen the soul from within me and that is the reason why I am heartless and unfeeling.

A monster.

"And you know what Lucan? I think so too. That's why I have a proposition for you.", She is back to staring at the sky.

"I'm listening." I'm genuinely curious about what she has to say, nothing good will come out of this conversation.

Of that I'm sure of.

"I know Andrea is your job, your task is to run her out of town back to New York.", she goes straight to the point. I'm about to ask how she found out when no-one, but the Volpe boss and I know, but she desperately interrupts me. — "Please, just listen to me." —For the first time since I have known Arianna, she has tears in her eyes, and she is trembling. — "I'm running out of time, dad just sold me to the highest bidder and from this day forward my life is not my own."

Even though she's my rival for the title of Capo, I can't refuse to help her. She's family even if it's not by blood. "What do you have in mind?" I know this alliance will end in disaster but at this very moment, I am all she has got.

"In this life, people will lose their morals and sell their souls to the devil for the right price. I asked around and offered money to Valeria Turner's employees at Valentina Co.", she sighs and looks ashamed, but also desperate. People do stupid shit when they don't see a way out of a shitty situation.

"I know just the thing that will break her and make her leave town for good."

If I were any other kind of man, I would help her and leave Andrea out of it, but I'm no prince and the principessa can save her fucking self.

"I'll help you get out of the arranged marriage but only if you tell me everything you know about Andrea Nicolasi. Every single detail that might help me get rid of her so I can complete my job and become head of the three families", I tell her with finality.

"You should know about what really happened to her mother." She gets lost in thought once again with a frown on her beautiful face. And I know that from this moment on everything will change.

Arianna proves just how cold-hearted and soulless she is when she reveals Andrea's hidden truths, and it is everything I need to break her spirit.

Maybe even her heart.

I have always been ruthless in the name of the Holy Trinity but if I go through with this there is no going back.

I will be just like my father.

Even worse, but I have no choice.

VENTUNO

COWARD

"Men do stupid things for women."
– Sansa Stark

TODAY IS MY SECOND TRAINING SESSION AND I FIND myself waiting for Rian in the Nicolasi home gym. The home gym is in the left wing of the mansion and it is huge with all kinds of fighting and exercise equipment.

I hope this day goes better than the last. He beat me until I almost passed out from the pain. My muscles still ache since the last time I was alone with him —and let's not forget the Irish bastard shot at me.

Rian is supposed to teach me one-on-one combat today and he was not happy about it. How do I know this? Well, the asshole was bitching all throughout our last session about how princesses should stay in their lane.

Misogynistic jerk.

In the meeting with all the other Holy Trinity brats, Benedetto explained how if I wanted to be head of three crime families, I should know how to handle a gun and defend myself against any threat. He doesn't know I've taken self-defense classes ever since I was almost kidnapped by one of my mom's crazy fans when I was ten years old. I was in Central Park with mom and I asked her for a cherry ice cone. I still remember how badly I wanted that ice cone because I couldn't stand how horrible the heat was that summer day in New York. She turned her back for a second and someone grabbed me. If it weren't for some random bystanders that got in the way of the man that was trying to take me away, lord knows what would have happened to me. From that moment on, she made sure I could protect myself in a situation where she wasn't there with me.

I would be lying if I say this life doesn't excite me, I always gravitated towards danger. I guess that's why every time I'm in the same vicinity as Lucan, my eyes always find him.

I won't even go there.

He's so not the guy for me.

I close the gym doors behind me, and I find the place empty. —This guy better not bail on me now. — I'm waiting for Rian to appear but there's no sight of him. It's way past the time we agreed on. From what I've observed in the amount of time I've been here, he's up with the fucking chickens.

I don't even think he sleeps.

I let my gaze wander around the room, and I can't believe they even own a fighting cage. There are guns, knives and all kinds of weapons hanging from the walls like trophies. They most likely keep it as souvenirs after they off someone. Seems like something Enzo, the sicko, might do.

I am in the middle of stretching when the gym door opens. "Finally, what took you so..." — *Why is God testing me today?* It isn't Rian standing in front of me, it's Lucan.

So besides him being a gigantic asshole, I should add stalker to his résumé. His mouth twitches and his eyes twinkle with mischief. "What the hell are you doing here?" — He's made it clear that he doesn't like me so why the hell is he always everywhere I'm at?

"Nobody gets to kick your ass but me, *principessa*." A sinister smile forms on his face.

"Oh, please I could take you any day." Shit, bad choice of words.

"Oh, baby I am counting on it." He grabs the hem of his shirt, pulls it over his head and now stands bare-chested before me. "But beg for my cock on another day. Today we fight."

Fuck. Me.

I've never seen a guy as hot as this one and I've been around plenty but no one like him. Lucan is too damn beautiful in a rugged and manly kind of way. He doesn't even try, and he looks completely fuck-able.

He radiates baby daddy energy that's for sure.

"Look, asshole I don't have time to waste and I'm expecting someone so get lost."

He completely ignores me and walks towards the fighting cage. Once he's inside he leaves the fence door open as an invitation for me to follow.

Yeah, no.

Pass.

"You're a lot of things, Andrea but I never took you for a coward. Your new dog is indisposed at the moment."

I ignore the jab towards Rian and focus on one word.

Coward?

He did not just call me a coward.

"What did you just call me?" I might be a lot of things, but a coward isn't one of them.

"You heard me or are you deaf too?" Out of nowhere he throws something in my direction.

I catch it as a reflex, and I inspect the item in my hands. A mouthguard.

He's looking for a fight.

I insert the mouthguard in my mouth and head to the fighting cage. "Let's go then."

He smiles while shaking his head like he finds me amusing. With a last glance in my direction, he turns around and begins to stretch his muscles and crack his fingers.

I climb into the cage and close the door with a loud clang.

He faces me with an eager look on his face. "Let's make it interesting." I don't like his tone. "If I win you have to do whatever I say for an entire day."

"And if I win, you'll get lost and never bother me again because quite frankly love, I am getting tired of seeing your face." I fire back.

"You know *principessa,* for someone as beautiful as you, you sure have one filthy mouth.", he smiles. "Now, shut the fuck up and give me your worst."

"That's all you'll ever get from me Volp..." I don't even get to finish the sentence before I'm thrown back into the cage's mattress.

This bitch.

This fucking bitch hit me.

I'm on my knees now and I touch my lips. I'm not surprised when I find blood coating my fingers. I don't give him another chance to hit me because I grab his balls and squeeze until he falls to the floor right next to me. I use the element of surprise in my favor and quickly rise from my spot on the floor until I am looking down on him. "I don't play fair love. Remember that the next time you put your unworthy hands on me."

"You little bit—", before he finishes his sentence my boot gets acquainted with his face.

That'll teach him to never... fucking...ever call me a coward.

Because although I am out of my element, with a family I can't trust and an uncertain future that involves crimes and lies, I won't stop fighting.

Never.

Not even when I know my end will come soon.

VENTIDUE

Tap Out

"You are not all evil, and I am not all good. Things are not that simple."
– Mary Margaret

Andrea

I KNOCKED HIM OUT TEN MINUTES AGO AND HE IS STILL unconscious on the cage's floor. I got scared for a minute there, I thought I had killed him, but thankfully he's waking up now.

Shit, I wanted to prove a point not to cause him severe damage but oh well, he brought it upon himself.

He's groaning now while trying to get up from the floor. He manages to stand up and face me, but his eyes are unfocused.

Oh…fuck…

Well, now I feel bad. That's a first for me.

"Look, I'm sorry but you kind of had it coming. If you would just" — I don't have time to finish the sentence before he grabs my head and puts me in a headlock.

What a sore fucking loser.

I try to fight him off but he's too strong. I try to knee him in the balls again because it's the only thing that works with this beast, but it is futile. I can feel my throat closing, my eyes watering. I can't breathe.

"Give up and tap out, *principessa*, I don't feel like going to a funeral.", he laughs.

If I tap out, then he has the pleasure of holding this against me for life. Fuck, my stubbornness will get me killed.

"Tap... the... fuck...out...

I'm almost to the point where I'll lose consciousness, but I manage to tap his arm twice.

He slowly turns me around to face him without letting go. I'm sure if he does, I will fall flat on the floor. However, he carries me out of the fighting cage with all the gentleness in the world. I'm too disoriented to pay attention to what he's doing but I feel his breath and the soft brush of his lips on my temple.

I must be hallucinating.

He puts me on my feet and brushes my hair out my face when he says: "Good girl, now get ready to go on a date with me tonight."

Huh? What the hell just happened? I fucking won.

"You did not win, Lucan. I knocked your ass out first." I remind him in case he has brain damage.

"Nah, *principessa*, you might have knocked me out, but the fight was far from over and I wasn't the one who tapped out." He must sense my confusion because he continues. "Now, go doll yourself up. I'm taking you somewhere classy tonight." He turns to leave but not before saying. "You made a deal Andrea, fucking honor it." With a grin on his face, he leaves with the last word. Great, I guess I have a date tonight, but I'll make him regret it.

VENTITRE

This Is No Fairytale

"I wish I had more time to seek out the dark forces and join their hellish crusade." - Morticia Addams

Lucan

IT'S BEEN A COUPLE OF HOURS SINCE THE HOT AS FUCK fighting session between Andrea and me. She would have never agreed to train with me or even be in the same room as me if I hadn't forced her hand. I don't even feel bad for the measures I had to take to make Rian, Benedetto's personal guard, not show up this morning at the gym to train Andrea.

I wouldn't have had to resort to roughing him up a bit and locking him in the guard's bathroom. He could have avoided all of it if he had just agreed to get lost for the day. So, if you think about it, it's actually his fault.

Goddamn it.

What the hell is it about this girl?

I mean, this girl is way too stubborn. Her smart mouth is somewhat annoying but, if I'm honest. that smart mouth and bratty attitude makes me rock hard.

I am Lucan Volpe, and the world will be mine for the taking, whether I want it or not. So, why does this girl have me coming back for more?

I steal a glance at her, she's slumped in the passenger seat looking at everything except me. Why do I want those hypnotizing brown eyes on me?

I am so fucked.

I pull up in front of Museum of Art of Detroit. This is my favorite place to be when the walls feel like they are closing in on me. This place means something to me; it's where my ma and I used to have our "special dates" like she used to call them. We would come here, and she would tell me all about the paintings, sculptures, and their meaning. She would also tell me what the artist was feeling when he or she created the piece. I found it truly fascinating, how someone with their two hands could create such beauty. There was this one piece made of glass that stuck with me. It was a little girl on her knees covering her ears, while terrifying creatures surrounded her.

I asked my mom that day what the artist was feeling while he made that piece. She said: "She's trying to silence the world, my love." My young self couldn't comprehend the meaning of her words but somehow, I could feel my ma's pain.

I wanted that.

I wanted to silence all the voices in my head.

The voices at home.

At that precise moment, I told my mother what I wanted to do with my life and asked her to buy me everything I needed because I too was going to create art. Art that would silence all the terrifying creatures that could one day hurt me. I won't ever forget the look in her eyes, not of disappointment but of sorrow.

She knew that would never be in the cards for me but still she bought me everything I thought I needed and even signed me up for art classes with my very own personal teacher. One day when I was six years old, my father came home early and found out about my new hobby. He showed me what he thought about it by breaking my hand and giving my mother a busted lip. That's when I learnt what my true purpose in this fucked up life was.

I shake the bad memories away because there's no use thinking about the past. I can't change it so why give it another thought? I stop the car and hand my keys to the valet guy, then jog over to the passenger door and offer my hand to Andrea.

She looks exquisite tonight. She's wearing a tight as fuck dress the color of her skin, it looks like it was painted on or some shit. All I know is she looks good enough to eat and I'm starving.

If I were any other type of man, I would tell her how stunning she looks tonight and if I had my sketchbook with me, I would love to translate such beauty onto paper.

But this is no fairytale and I'm no prince.

VENTIQUATTRO

JUST PRETEND

"Money makes me romantic."
– Audrey Hepburn

Andrea

OUT OF ALL THE PLACES I COULD IMAGINE THIS Neanderthal taking me for our date, I would've never expected it to be an art museum.

I've been on all kinds of dates before - roller skating, movies, restaurants, but this is new for me.

Lucan rented the entire museum for the night.

There's no one here but the two of us.

This is too intimate.

I can't hide here.

The museum of Art of Detroit is beautiful. I mean, it's no Louvre but the paintings and sculptures on display here are truly magnificent.

For some reason Lucan is quiet here and acting strange. Not that he acts normal by any means but here he is almost vulnerable. It's no fun kicking someone when they're down. I was planning to give him hell on this date but how can I when he looks like someone just murdered his puppy?

Yeah, weird. I know.

He arranged a private tour of the museum and the guide told us all about the art pieces that are displayed here. There's one piece in particular that catches my eye and I near it to get a closer look. My heart shrinks in my chest because of what I'm seeing before me.

It's a sculpture of a tiny girl covering her ears while there are monsters hovering over her. I get a closer look at the label, it reads. "*Nascondersi dai mostri.*" - I'm sure I butchered the name.

"Hiding from monsters." Lucan whispers in my ear. I didn't even notice him joining my side.

I'm still staring in awe at the sculpture before me. "It's so tragically beautiful." I feel so connected to this piece. It's like someone crawled into the deepest part of my soul and discovered my biggest fear.

The little girl seems so scared and lonely.

"Indeed, it is.", he murmurs so softly that I almost miss it.

Almost.

I turn my head in his direction expecting to see him admiring the beauty before us but, instead, I find him gazing at me. His eyes tell me one thing, but his actions say otherwise.

Ugh! One day with him and I'm already so confused and starting to lower my guard.

This is bad.

This is really bad.

I can't afford to do that.

At least not now.

Especially not with him.

"The terrified girl symbolizes the artist and the ugly beasts hovering above her represent the world.", he pauses, admiring the piece. "Well, that's one of many interpretations."

I am curious now. "There's more than one?", I ask.

"Yes, some say the sculptor suffered from schizophrenia and the girl is him and the beasts are the monsters from his past. He committed suicide right after he finished this piece. He didn't even get to see it being displayed."

Lucan's tone is eerily calm and sad.

"How do you know this?", I ask him while still looking at that sculpture of the hunted girl.

He shrugs "I know art."

Yeah, there's more to it than that.

"Come, the night is not over yet.", he says before holding his hand for me to take.

We don't have to be enemies, at least not tonight.

So, I take his hand, and just for tonight I pretend.

I pretend that I'm not an orphan.

I pretend that I'm just a normal girl with a normal boy on a beautiful date.

Just pretend.

THE NIGHT IS ALMOST OVER, AND I HAVEN'T FELT THIS AT peace in a year. I wish every night could be like this.

I wish this feeling would never end, but it will.

It always does.

I don't know how Lucan pulled it off but, inside the constellation exhibit he had someone prepare us dinner. It looks like the inside of a beautiful Italian restaurant.

We are literally dining under the stars.

He has been quiet all throughout dinner and surprisingly I enjoy the silence. I don't mind his presence as much as I thought I would. I might be losing it, maybe that explains why I ask what's been on my mind since the moment Fallon told me. How does he deal with her lost?

"How did it feel like?" I ask. "Losing her, I mean?", I ask but I know I won't get an answer. There's no way Lucan will confide in me.

A stranger.

An enemy.

A couple of uncomfortable seconds pass before he surprises the hell out of me with his answer.

"It felt like every goodbye ever said to me all at once." That's it. That's all he offers me before he continues eating like this moment never happened.

Huh.

We carry on in silence, but I keep replaying his answer in my head. How could a mother leave her kids and never look back? My mom would've never done such a thing, only death tore us apart. She had no choice, but Lucan's mother chose her freedom over her kids.

I'm almost done with my plate when Lucan asks: "If you could be anywhere in the world right now, where would you be?" I didn't expect small talk from him but alright.

If I had one wish, I would choose to be wherever my mom is, but I'm not telling him that.

"New York is where my heart is.", I tell him truthfully.

Lucan drops his fork but keeps a hold on his knife which he is holding with so much force that, although it is scientifically impossible, he could break it. He just might.

"I wasn't aware you had a special someone at home.", his tone is that of a jealous man.

"Why would you be aware of that Lucan? You don't know me." It's the truth.

Nobody here knows me except for Fallon. Everyone made their minds up about me according to what they see on gossip sites or just from what their parents tell them. No one has taken the time to ask me what I want or how I feel. So, yeah, they don't know shit about me. They just assume.

He abruptly stands up from his chair and says: "You're right, I don't."

Date over. It was nice while it lasted.

VENTICINQUE

Love At First Sight

"You know, I'm getting pretty damn tired of everybody."
– Lip Gallagher

Andrea

The Past

"SUNSHINE, DID I EVER TELL YOU HOW I MET YOUR FATHER?" Mom says while sowing my costume for my school's winter recital. I don't like dancing, but the look on mama's face when I dance is pure happiness.

It makes me happy.

My mommy should smile more, she only ever does it for me.

"Is it like Cinderella when she met her prince?" My innocent question makes her laugh. Her laugh is my favorite sound, when I hear it, I know all is right in my world.

"No, my love. It was even more magical," she tells me, and a grin takes over her pretty face.

"But, mom, what can be more magical than a fairytale?" I ask.

"Life. It was real life, sunshine, and that makes it even better than any fairytale", she beams. "You see, Andrea, princesses don't write their own happily ever after and they don't get to choose their prince. The author does and once the book is done, it's over. In real life though, you can write your own story, choose your prince and the book keeps going

as long as your heart beats." I look up and meet my mother's gaze. It's filled with so much emotion and love. Why does she still feel love for my daddy? He broke her heart when he abandoned us.

"I met your father one cold winter night in New York city. I had two jobs, you see, so I worked late shifts. I was in a hurry back home before your grandparents started getting worried. Back then it was dangerous for a young girl to walk alone at night. I lived in a really bad area in Brooklyn."

"I was two blocks away from my house when I heard a man's painful grunts from behind a dumpster. My gut was telling me it was not safe to stop and help a stranger. I didn't know what he did to be in that position or if it was just a ruse to get me to stop and hurt me in any way, but my heart, the fool, made me stop and help the strange man. I walked closer to him and was left speechless."

I've heard of love at first sight, but I never believed in it, until that very moment. This handsome man with beautiful indigo eyes and hair as black as the dead sky was staring at me with pain and wonder in his gaze. Don't ask me how I knew that he was the one for me, maybe it was my naive heart, but at that moment I knew he was my person."

"Mommy, what happened next?" I'm eager to know more about their first encounter, more about my daddy.

She goes on to tell me the rest of the story, how he told her his name was Charles Nolan and he was mugged on his way back to his apartment. Her tone changes when she tells me this part of their story.

It hurt her; my daddy hurt her heart.

"I spent a week nursing him back to health and hiding him in my family's attic. We talked about our childhoods and our dreams. I should've known that something was not right when he refused to talk about his family. I just thought it was a sore subject and I wanted to respect his wishes. I fell in love with that man with every word and every

gesture of love he gave me. - Mommy stops and takes a deep breath - "Nunca nadie me había demostrado amor como el lo hizo, mi niña." No one had ever shown me love like he did, my girl.

"Did he really love you, mommy?" It's barely a whisper.

I don't want to hurt her. I just want to understand.

"Very much so, my girl, of that I have no doubt.", she smiles while touching a gold chain with the letters VAL. My mother had plenty of designer jewelry but that necklace, which looked so inexpensive and like it could break at any given moment, was her favorite. Her most prized possession after me, she used to say.

I finally feel brave enough to ask. "Why did he leave us? "Didn't he want me?"

"Oh, my sweet Andrea, he loved you with his entire heart and soul." Mommy hugs me tightly to her chest. "Andrea, he did it to protect us, all of us. He—"

Present

BANG!

A loud noise wakes me from the most pleasant sleep I have had since I lost mom. I look at my alarm clock and it reads 3:34 am. What was that? I thought about ignoring the loud noises coming from downstairs and going back to sleep, but the shouts of two angry men have me rising from my bed as quickly as possible and heading downstairs. I should stay in bed, I know, but my curiosity wins over my good judgment.

After the long day I had yesterday with almost being choked to death and being wined and dined by the same guy who did said choking. You might say all I want is to fall into a deep slumber and not wake up for days. However, the ruckus downstairs won't let me.

I walk down the long stairs and follow the loud shouts. It seems to be coming from Benedetto's home office. The door is not all the way closed and I can clearly see two men facing off.

Benedetto and Uncle Cassius.

"You promised!" — Uncle Cassius shouts. "Don't do this to her."

"Keep your voice down.", Benedetto hisses. "Andrea can't know. Nobody, for that matter, can find out of your betrayal to this family. - *Il tuo tradimento a tuo fratello.*", he gets up from his chair and heads to the window, giving Cassius his back.

"You know damn well why I got rid of him", he sounds angry now. "They were mi—" Benedetto rudely interrupted him. "Shut your goddamn mouth! Not only did you betray this family, but you also killed my son!", he screams. Not caring at all if he wakes everyone in this house or if I overhear the devastating secret. "You killed my boy." Benedetto silently sobs.

I can't believe this.

Cassius killed my dad.

He never got the chance to raise me because he was murdered by his own blood. Why does this hurt so bad? Maybe because this man not only caused my mother pain, but he also left me without a father.

"I am your boy too." Cassius sounds contempt.

Grandfather walks back to his desk and stands before Cassius. "You stopped being my son the moment you pointed the gun at your brother's head and stole his bride. The only reason you are still breathing is because of those two boy's upstairs and, as for Andrea, she will fulfill her father's wishes." There's a long pause before he continues. "She will be the boss of this family; it is her duty. Her whore of a mother had no right to keep her from us." I watch as Cassius grabs Benedetto by his throat and holds him up against the study's wall.

"You damn well know that she's..." —Uncle Cassius growls in his face and tightens his hold on Benedetto's neck. But before he can refute his father's accusations against him, he is interrupted yet again.

"I won't tell you again to shut your goddamn mouth." – Benedetto struggles getting the words out but still he threatens. — "Andrea will never know that you killed her father with the help of that whore!"

I quickly cover my mouth before a shocked gasp escapes me.

My instinct is telling me to barge in and demand answers, but that's reckless and won't guarantee me the truth from them. I am not only living under the same roof as liars and criminals, but also a fucking murderer of the worst kind.

Uncle Cassius committed the worst sin against his own flesh and blood.

Now, more than ever I shouldn't trust anyone, not even my goddamn blood.

VENTISEI

Well Played Asshole

"I'm fine. I'm just being dramatic. It's what I do." – Lorelai Gilmore

Andrea

Eighteen years old

TODAY IS BITTERSWEET.

My first birthday without mom.

Roberta surprised me with breakfast in bed ordered by my grandfather. He also sent a dozen pink roses and filled my room with balloons. Well, he didn't do shit. He asked his employees to do it for him.

I haven't seen or heard from him since the horrifying revelation of the crimes committed against my father and the accusation against my mother. I've been avoiding everyone by staying in my room all weekend.

Not that anyone noticed.

That night I watched Uncle Cassius getting in his car and leaving like a thief in the night from my bedroom window. I haven't seen or heard from him since.

I don't know how I'll react the next time I see him. This man is the reason my mother suffered so much in life.

I will probably cut out his heart and give it to his sons.

What am I going to do now?

Benedetto knew all along that my father didn't leave us willingly. He also has his son's killer living under the same roof as me. Why keep that a secret from me? What does he want?

And why would he say that mom helped kill him? That's a reach since Valeria Turner wouldn't have hurt a fly, let alone the love of her life.

I knew this would happen.

I am surrounded by secrets and betrayals.

Should I confront Benedetto and demand to know the truth about my parents? But what guarantee do I have that he will tell me the truth?

No. It's up to me to find out the truth.

Since my mother's passing, I've come to terms that it is me against the world now. But how am I supposed to let this go? Why should they go on living life like they didn't cause my family so much pain? And how can I make these people pay for their crimes when it feels like everything, she told me was a lie?

Fuck, this hurts.

What also hurts is that the day I've been anxiously waiting for has arrived. I am finally eighteen years old and I can leave this town for good. Now that I know for certain that this family caused my parents so much pain, I don't want anything to do with them. I didn't want to be boss before and I certainly don't want to lead this family now. How can they expect me to be the head of a family I don't trust or hold any respect for?

Let the twins kill each other for it.

Benedetto knew he couldn't possibly hold me here against my will. The moment I turn eighteen, I am no longer under his temporary custody. He has no hold over me.

Did he want me here because he wanted to get to know me? He seemed sincere the night he gave me my dad's photo, but then he insulted my dead mother and accused her of murder. There's more to it if that I am sure. He held so much animosity against my mother and he didn't want anything to do with me before, so why now?

Fuck.

I don't understand any of this. It can't be money he's after. He must be bathing in hundred dollar bills every night. He must have a motive for all of this and in my gut, I feel it is a sinister one.

What is he hiding?

I am running out of time, the moment the court agrees to hand me over my inheritance and the board of shareholders appoint me CEO of Valentina, I am out of here.

I won't finish school here. The only good thing about this place is coming with me to New York as soon as she graduates.

I can't lose Fallon, right now she's all I have, and I need her in my corner. I have a feeling shit's about to get real and I'm barely eighteen years old.

My phone pings with a message from a number I don't recognize.

Unknown number: Come down.

Me: Who is this?

Unknown number: I'm waiting.

I leave my bed and walk to my window; Lucan's Maserati is parked in the driveway. I haven't heard from him since our "date" last Friday night. The asshole just ended the date and dropped me off at the mansion.

Me: I don't think so. Go away.

I send the middle finger emoji for dramatic effect.

I plug my phone into its charger and start my morning routine. I have a lot to figure out today.

What's my next move?

I'm almost done curling my hair into stylish waves when there's a knock at the door.

"Ms. Nicolasi, Mr. Volpe wishes to speak with you." Roberta tells me with a scowl on her face.

She's always so proper and it's obvious she doesn't approve of me.

Like I give a fuck what she thinks.

I'm done caring about what others do or say.

"I'll be done in a minute." I dismiss her because honestly, I'm no in the mood for her shit.

I take my time getting dressed and head downstairs. Benedetto is nowhere in sight. I bet he doesn't think I know what he's been hiding. I have a gut feeling and it's telling me not to trust him. The only thing in my favor is that no one knows I heard their conversation. No one knows I was there that night and listed to their argument. Now I know what they've all been hiding.

I have to keep it that way. I've watched enough crime movies to know that the first one to blab is the first one that gets buried.

Benedetto protected a murderer and is now trying to keep me here under false pretenses. He doesn't want to get to know his long-lost granddaughter. He just wants me here to be the face of his fucked up criminal organization all the while protecting my father's killer.

Oh, and let's not forget he called my mom a whore and accused her of murder.

I find Lucan waiting for me at the bottom of the stairs. He looks different, not at all like the pretentious asshole he truly is. He almost looks carefree, wearing jeans and a white plain t-shirt. His hair is styled differently too, not perfect like usual.

"You look beautiful.", he smiles and offers his hand for me to take.

Yeah, I don't think so.

"I think my text message was pretty clear." I don't have time for this. "I don't want to be around you. Not today."

I'm done playing his games.

One day he threatens me, the next he kisses me, he chokes me and then takes me out on a date.

What the hell.

He must think I'm the president of the dumb hoe club. — "I said no, what part of that don't you understand?"

What he pulls out of his jeans' pocket makes my blood turn cold. No, it can't be.

I touch my neck, feeling for the only thing that gives me peace and it's not there.

Oh God, no.

How did he get a hold of my necklace?

I've been so busy with self-pity and wallowing that I completely forgot mom's necklace. I'm always so careful and I never take it off.

Fuck!

The last time I had it with me was in the training session.

"How did you get that? Give it back!" I snap.

I have so much pent-up rage that I'm losing control of my

emotions. I'm a fucking mess, but that necklace grounds me, it feels like mom.

Like home.

"I'll give it back, only if you spend a day with me." He must be joking.

This can't be happening right now.

"Please, just give it back." I try to reason with him, but I know it is futile. There's nothing reasonable about Lucan Volpe. He studies me with an unreadable expression on his face.

Yeah, he's not giving it back if I don't do as he says.

Feeling defeated for the first time since I arrived in this town, I give in and do as he says. I can't risk losing the necklace and this psycho is capable of choking me with it. "Fine, one day, but give me your word that when the day is over, you'll give it back."

"You have my word, Andrea." he looks me down with an intense look on his face. His tone is not sarcastic or condescending, it's honest.

Well, that's a first.

I can't believe I just agreed to spend a whole day with this idiot. Out of everything I needed to do today, this wasn't it. I need to call Emilio and ask for an update on my mother's company. Last I heard the board of directors is demanding a meeting with me. Apparently, I am too young to be the CEO of a global enterprise. I also need to ask him some questions about mom. I think no one knew her better than him.

Maybe Lucan is a welcome distraction after all.

I also notice he calls me Andrea; He is the only one that does besides Benedetto. I'm curious as to why.

"Why don't you call me Drea like everyone else?"

"One day soon you'll learn that I'm not everyone else.", he

grabs my hand and leads us out of the mansion. "Let's go, every second of your day is mine. We can't waste them."

I pride myself on being a strong and independent woman that takes no shit from men...today, I fail.

In my defense, he has the only thing that means the world to me. This means I'm at his mercy.

Well played asshole, well played.

VENTISETTE

What Are You Doing To Me?

"Wow, we really are bitches."
– Rachel Green

Andrea

STUCK IN THE TWILIGHT ZONE.

That's the only way I can describe my day with Lucan.

After we left grandfather's mansion, we had breakfast at a small and cozy diner in town. I thought it would feel awkward and uncomfortable since I'm a hostage and all but, if I'm being honest, it was kind of pleasant. Lucan made me forget that my mother is gone, my father was murdered by my uncle and my grandfather is a piece of shit.

Lucan has taken an interest in my life, but I'm not naive. I know he just wants leverage that he can use against me later on.

"Were you close with your mom?" he suddenly asks.

I'm not surprised by the question because my mom's death was all over the news. I just want to forget, just for today. Not forget her but forget that the person that meant the most to me is lost to me forever.

"Change the subject, Lucan. I don't want to talk about her." I really can't, not today, and especially not with him.

He wants me gone and the only thing that could truly hurt me is people finding out the cause of my mother's death. "What's the plan for today?", I ask to change the focus back on him.

He leans back on the booth we are occupying, looking at me like he wants to crawl inside me and lay claim to every single part of me. That's the thing about Lucan. He doesn't need words, his eyes tell me everything I need to know, and right now, he looks like he wants me.

He wants this day with me, but why? What's his endgame?

He feels his pants looking for something and pulls out a cigarette. He does it again but this time it's for a zippo with an ugly snake on it.

Huh.

Who would've thought, the student body president and chess geek... smokes?

He lights up the cigarette, but he's not paying attention to it. He's lost in thought. So, I leaned over the booth, reached over, and pluck the cigarette out of his mouth. I take a drag and quickly blow a great amount of smoke right in his face. That makes him snap out of it and he trains those baby blues on me.

Yeah, that got his attention.

He takes the cigarette from me and scowls. "Get up, we're going shopping." he tells me while dropping a couple of fifties before rising from his seat and exiting the diner, leaving me to follow.

This guy has no manners whatsoever but, thankfully, breakfast is over.

One more second this close to him and I will fall on my knees for traitorous Judas.

* * *

I'm relatively new to this place so I don't judge it much. Detroit is different but some of the people that I have met thus far are over the top and way too pretentious for my taste. The fashion business prepared me for this but still I was not expecting rude as fuck criminals. Even so, I can't deny the appeal. The streets are squeaky clean, there's no hellish traffic and I haven't seen a single paparazzi insight since I arrived here.

The opposite of New York.

Still, I wouldn't willingly trade my city for this place.

We are currently inside one of the most expensive boutiques in town by the looks of it. The walls are painted matte black, the mannequins are made of glass, the ceiling is one big ass mirror, and I won't even get into the women that work here.

They look way too perfect.

One approaches us with a knowing smile on her face. "Lucan, good to see you again." I don't appreciate her tone and I hate the feeling of possessiveness that runs through my body.

He is mine.

Well, only for the day and I don't share my toys.

"Leah, we need a short evening dress for Andrea. The cost won't be a problem.", he tells her before he leaves and goes who knows where.

"Come with me darling. We'll find the perfect dress to bring that boy to his knees.", she winks and guides me to the changing rooms. Even the changing rooms are elegant, with gold chandeliers on the ceiling and mirrors everywhere.

"We need a dress that will accentuate your beautiful curves. Here, try this one.", she hands me an elegant red, satin dress that stops just above the knee.

She leaves me to try the dress on. I quickly change into it and stare at my reflection in the mirror.

I look hot. Leah was right, this dress hugs all my curves and pushes my breasts up, making them look fake. I take my phone out to snap some mirror selfies for Fallon, but before I can do that someone knocks.

"It's occupied." I call out.

The dressing room's door opens before I can stop the person on the other side and Lucan walks in. "I said it's occupied, get out.", he shuts the door behind him and closes in on me until my back hits the mirror.

I follow his gaze and notice he's staring at us... staring at our reflection.

I look up and I'm surprised by the look in his eyes. It's the look of a hunter waiting to devour his prey.

"What are you doing to me, principessa?", he rasps and in one swift move he grabs my ass and lifts me up until my back hits the dressing room wall. "Whatever you're doing, stop it. I am not a man to be played with.", he snarls.

My heart is beating abnormally fast and it feels like it's trying to escape out of my chest and crawl towards him.

Pathetic I know, but this stupid need for him is clouding my judgement. Blame it on the past couple of shitty days.

"Shut up and kiss me." I grab his ass and pull him to me.

"Whatever the *principessa* wants, she shall get.", he flashes me a charming smile before taking my mouth in his and devouring it.

Just one look from him and he sets my damn body on fire. I'm tired of fighting it, maybe I should give in and see if I can bring this king to his knees.

Lucan's mouth leaves mine. I think he's about to stop this but then he surprises me by trailing soft kisses down my neck.

I'm so lost in him that I didn't even notice him dropping down on his knees. I feel his hands roaming my body like he's trying to discover a secret only my body could tell him.

I'm lost in thought staring at his lips, wanting them on me, on every part of my body. "Don't you dare stop now." I growl. I'm so lost in pleasure that I don't even care that I'm acting like a needy bitch.

Lucan looks up at me with a knowing grin. "Oh, baby girl, I wasn't planning on it."

We both know it's too late to turn back now, this fucked up train with no destination has left the tracks.

Time stops as I feel his hands on my waist, goosebumps travel all over my body when I feel his breath on my navel. Lucan leisurely hikes up my dress until my red thong is exposed. Thank God, I wasn't lazy today and decided to match my underwear.

"Hold the dress up."

A shudder grips me at the authority in his tone. I do as he says and slide the dress up revealing my stomach. His fingers trail down my body, leaving goosebumps in their wake. Then he cups me through my underwear.

I'm wet as fuck and he knows it too.

Lucan drags a finger down my wet folds. The sensation sends electricity running through my body.

God, his hands feel so good.

He thrusts two fingers inside me in one go and I can't stop myself from moaning his name. The sound of his skin against my arousal is driving me insane with need.

He leaves love bites on each of my thighs and kisses me everywhere except where I need him most.

Oh, hell no.

I grab a handful of his hair and make him look up at me. "Taste me, Lucan." I bet he can tell how badly I need him with the flushed look on my face and my needy tone.

He looks at me with a predatory grin on his handsome face and he does just that.

The king fell to his knees for this queen.

Checkmate, bitch.

VENTOTTO

A Match Made In Hell

"If you need some love, get a hooker."
– Paris Geller

FUCK ME.

This was a ruse to try and get some useful leverage on my enemy, not to have her stick her tongue down my throat and for me to stick my mouth on her perfect, sinful pussy.

That's a lie.

I have everything I need to run her out of the city, but ever since my meet-up with Arianna, I can't sleep. I now know what haunts her dreams and what makes her heart bleed. With that bit of information, I can prove she's unfit to rule the Nicolasi family, let alone three crime families.

Am I ready to do this though? To ruin this girl that in just a matter of weeks has turned my life upside down and for the better?

She makes me feel and want things that I shouldn't.

They're not in the cards for me.

It is too late.

The things I wanted before I turned into my father's son.

Before I became a liar, a cheat...a murderer.

Every moment with her makes me feel and that's something I can't afford to do. People want you until something better comes along and then they drop you like you meant nothing. My mother proved to me that nothing good comes from loving and needing someone other than yourself. They take a piece of you when they leave, and nothing fills that void. I tried to fix the hurt my mother's abandonment did to my soul by drinking, smoking and fucking everything in sight but nothing ever really made me forget how it felt to have the one person in this world that should love and care for me unconditionally, leave without an ounce of regret and never look back.

Andrea makes me forget. I feel at peace whenever she's nearby.

She's my muse.

She challenges me. Every time I push her, she pushes back ten times harder. It's sick and twisted this thing that is growing between us. Now that I've had my first taste of her... there's no stopping it.

I want all of her.

I want to fucking own her.

I look at her, truly look at her in this moment, with her skin flushed, her beautiful blonde hair sticking out in all directions, and that hot as fuck red dress. She looks like sex on legs.

This little devil does things to me and I'm tired of fighting it because there's no escaping her.

And there's no escaping me.

I stare into her eyes. I'm not a guy of many words but what I feel for this girl, words can't express.

I know it's not love, it's something primal and dark...it's obsession. She consumes my every thought, in a room filled with strangers I can sense her, feel her.

Only ever her.

I get off my knees and face her. "You're fucking everything up principessa." I can't think with her this close to me.

I need to gather my thoughts and I can't do that while she's giving me those hot as hell fuck-me- eyes. "Get the dress and let's go.", I turn my back on her and leave. It's almost painful to leave her at this point.

I'm so fucked.

I pass a few salesgirls and ignore their knowing eyes. I'm pretty sure everyone heard Andrea's cries of pleasure, but I really don't give a fuck.

Let everyone know.

She's mine.

I take a cigarette out and light it up. I breathe the smoke in and slowly inhale towards the sky. It's almost nighttime, there's one more place we need to go to. I reach for my phone and dial the one person that can help me now. "Hey, big brother," Gia answers cheerfully. "I need you to do something for me *topolina*, we're on our way." I tell her, while I watch Andrea through the store's window.

"We? You and...?", she asks with a curious tone, clearly wanting to know more.

I tell her the truth. "Andrea and I."

Just like that I end the call.

In the short amount of time, I have spent with this girl, she has silenced all my demons. Before her all I saw was black but somehow in the mist of all the chaos and darkness around me she managed to add color into my fucked-up life. In one day, everything changed and all my plans for her did as well.

I don't know how I will find a way to save my sisters and keep the girl too. Tommaso will have to find a way to deal with her presence in this city.

Andrea's role in my fucked-up game has changed. She is engraved in my brain and I can't shake her. It's like a sickness and I don't want the fucking cure.

She's not the pawn...not anymore.

She's the motherfucking queen.

VENTINOVE

No One's Trophy Wife

"If she doesn't scare you, no evil thing will."
– Cruella De Vil

Arianna

COLD HEARTED BITCH.

That's what they all call me behind my back. They pretend to like me, follow me and some even admire me, but they don't.

I'm rotten.

They know it.

Most importantly, I know it.

I am my mother's daughter after all.

I have never hidden who I am, never pretended to be anything but my fucking fabulous self. That is the reason I feel no guilt when I disappoint them. I never misled them, they just looked at my angelic appearance and decided that is who I am.

A fallen angel, perhaps.

When I was younger, I wanted to be "normal". Whatever the hell that is nowadays. I wanted to not feel envy every time my little sisters did something to impress my mother. I wanted — no I needed— to not feel empty every time my baby sister told me she loved me and wanted snuggles. I wanted to show her that I cared, but it was difficult for me.

It has always been difficult to be like everyone else.

The matter of fact is, I just wanted to be like them. Well, maybe not exactly like them because Mila is too damn naive and Kadra is well... an unlikeable bitch.

Someone hurt her and that was the final nail in my coffin. I might not care about much in life, but I care about them. If I had a heart which I do not, it would beat just for them.

But that was before...before I was sold like a piece of filthy cattle to the highest bidder.

Senator Kenton of Washington, DC.

Fifty-four years old widow and father of three. That old sick fuck bought me, and my father did not even think twice before signing the contract.

Gabriele is punishing me.

He gave me my task and I refused. Out of all the days to be fucking selfish I went against my nature and fucked up.

But I couldn't do it.

I couldn't do that to my sister.

So now I am paying the price.

My new husband paid for a young hot and submissive wife.

Those were his demands.

Submissive.

I'll show the old fuck, exactly who I am.

I am no one's fucking trophy wife.

My thoughts are interrupted by Giana. — "What did you say? Sorry I wasn't paying attention.", I tell her.

"I think Luc really likes Andrea." Oh no. If the idiot falls for her then there's no chance in hell, he'll help me get out of this mess.

Fuck!

"What makes you say that?" I need to know.

How will this change things?

"He's just acting weird lately. For example, he just called and asked me to contact a sleazy gossip website and stop a story that they are running on Andrea. You don't do shit like that unless you care about someone."

No-no-no.

That was my only move.

I feel it creeping in and corrupting my every thought. I never could control when I was young and now that I'm older… it's ten times worse.

Envy.

Rage.

Hurt.

Another person that doesn't put me first.

I am his friend, and he chooses her?

You chose wrong, Lucan.

So-fucking-wrong.

I make a move for her phone. — "If you want, I can do it for you. I know the chief editor and I'm sure she'll definitely stop the story if I ask her to."— I smile at my friend.

My only friend and after tonight?

My ex-friend for sure.

Fuck, I'm scum.

But if no one will save me.

I'll do it my fucking self.

TRENTA

MONSTERS

"It says here you're a bitch."
- Salem

Andrea

THAT ASSHOLE.

Now I understand why half the women population at Holy Trinity Academy is enamored with Lucan. Not only is he gorgeous, but he can charm the panties of anyone and if that's not enough his tongue can bring any woman to their knees.

He made me come in a matter of seconds just with his tongue.

Jesus, but that tongue of his almost made me profess my undying devotion to him. I'm no virgin. I've had boyfriends and meaningless hookups before, but nothing felt like this.

Like him.

It felt real.

I fix myself, leaving no evidence of what just transpired between us before stepping out of the dressing room. Once I do, I see that Leah is waiting for me at the checkout counter. Something stops me in my tracks, a dress on the window's mannequin. I can feel the dress calling out to me, crazy I know, but it's just that perfect.

It's a short silver dress. The material is satin and a bit see-through. "It's fabulous, isn't it?" I hear the sales lady whisper behind me. "It would look so good on you", she's paid to say whatever she needs to in order to make a sale, but I still appreciate the compliment. She's not lying though; it would look great on me.

I walk closer to the mannequin and asked what I wanted to know since the moment she directed a word at Lucan. "How do you know Lucan?" I turn around and face her. I can tell she finds me amusing because a soft laugh escapes her mouth. "Put your claws away darling, I know him through his father Tommaso." I know there's more she's not telling me. "Now, are you taking both dresses?" I can't believe I got jealous over him.

Fucking Lucan.

"Yeah, charge it to his card." I grab the bags and head out the door where Lucan is waiting for me. I have no explanation for why I bought the second dress, but I have a feeling I might get to use it against him later.

WE HAVE JUST ARRIVED AT THE LAST DESTINATION FOR the day.

The Volpe mansion.

This place is crazy. If I thought my grandfather's home was extra and ridiculously expensive, the Volpe mansion is out of this world. The decorations are all black and white, with classic paintings hanging on the walls. In the middle of the living room, there's a family portrait. I walk towards it to get a closer look. There's an older, handsome man that I'm assuming is Tommaso Volpe, Lucan's father. He is holding Cara's hand in the picture but not Giana's.

Weird.

Lucan is also in the portrait standing behind his father looking like the devil himself before he fell from grace.

Strong, powerful, and sinfully beautiful. There's so much anger in his stare though. It's clear to see and the artist captured it beautifully.

The moment we arrived at his house, Lucan went off to find his sister Giana and gave me free rein to explore his home. So that's what I've been doing for the past couple of minutes.

His home feels cold and if I'm honest, not very family oriented.

My body completely stills when I hear someone clearing their throat to announce their arrival. "And who might you be?", a man asks from behind me with an arrogant tone.

Lucan's dad.

Shit.

I turn around and face him. I'm not afraid of him, like I'm not afraid of his son. But he is an intimidating man, and he vibrates the same dark and powerful energy as Lucan.

There's no doubt this man created him.

The Volpe boss is an immaculate man with the same light brown hair as his son. The only difference between them is their eyes. Lucan has clear blue eyes and Tommaso's are a light shade of green.

His intense gaze is trained on me. Maybe he thinks I'm about to bolt out of here like some scared little girl. Oh, how wrong he is. "I think we both know who I am, Mr. Volpe." I look him dead in the eye. "Let's not play games."

From the dark and furious look that crosses his face, I know he didn't like my disrespectful tone.

Tough shit.

"Very well, Miss Turner.", his chilling tone makes me shiver. There's something cold and sinister about this man, not even his son gives out this kind of vibe. "What are you doing with my son?", the way he says my son makes it seem like he thinks of Lucan as a piece of property and I'm a threat.

"Well, isn't that the million-dollar question. I wish I could answer you Tommaso, but I don't know the answer." Fuck, if I don't want to be seeing mom anytime soon, I should really shut my mouth. "I'm his hostage today. He brought me here, so maybe when he comes down you can ask him yourself."

And there I go again with my big mouth.

Oh well.

Tommaso is studying my every movement with his beady, cold eyes, like he's waiting for me to slip and confess all my sins. Hell will freeze over before I tell the grim reaper himself my deepest and darkest secret, the one that haunts me in my dreams and keeps me from dreaming of a better life. You see, the same evil that took my mother from me, will eventually come for me. I can't fight it... it will win.

Monsters always do.

I can see his displeasure with my nonchalant response. Clearly, he expected a different reaction, but even when I am hurt, scared or fucking agitated, I will never give them the response they want. It shows weakness and cowardice and that's something I am not. Tommaso opens his mouth to say something back but before he does, something behind me catches his attention.

I feel him before I see him. His powerful and commanding presence is hard to miss.

Hmmm...what makes a father, a powerful one, fear his own son?

I'm caught between two monsters but the one behind me seems like the one I should fear the most. Tommaso shows his ugly with no apologies or shame, you know what to expect from that monster but his son? Lucan only shows what he wants people to see. With his god-awful good looks and charming personality, he can fool anyone.

But when you do meet the darkness within him...may God help your soul.

"Stay away from her, I won't warn you again.", his words are filled with disdain.

Lucan grabs my hand and rushes me out the door.

"Wait, why did you bring me here?" I'm confused.

He doesn't stop until we're out of his house.

"I needed to ask my sister something, don't worry about it. Let's go, I'll take you home."

"You couldn't ask her over the phone? You really had to drive all of the way down here?" I don't believe him for a second, he's hiding something.

He grabs my face and gently presses his forehead to mine. "Happy birthday, *principessa*.", he winks before he steps back and goes to the driver's side.

"How did you know today's my birthday?"

"I know everything about you.", he winks. "Now get your sexy ass in my car, you need to get ready."

What?

"Ready for what?" I didn't want anyone to know today is my birthday, but who am I kidding? If Benedetto didn't tell them, then every article and post online about my eighteenth birthday would've.

Great.

I hate this damn day

TRENTUNO

My Brother

"I am not crazy. My mother had me tested."
– Sheldon Lee Cooper

Lorenzo

SOCIOPATH.

Antisocial personality disorder. The nice doctor my father hired to "fix me" tries to explain. There's no fixing me. Not this late in the game. I knew there was something different about me from a very young age. When I would use to sit for hours listening through the door while my father tortured grown men until they begged for mercy that never came.

I don't feel like others do. Nothing holds my interest for too long and when it does, I obsess over it to the point it consumes my every thought.

You see, my brother Val and I are identical twins. When we were first born nobody could tell us apart and our father was so lost in a bottle of Jack that it was a miracle whenever he noticed us at all.

Val has always been quiet, always hiding in the shadows and never really caring about anything or anyone, except for me. I know my brother loves me and I would do anything for him.

That's how I know I'm not all gone.

That's a good thing. I may not care for anything in this fucked up world, but I do care about my brother.

Do I love him? I don't know, but I don't like it when he hurts and I would destroy anyone or anything that threatens him.

Valentino is the one thing that keeps me from going over the edge. From losing control and self-destructing. That's what I do and have always done. I ruin anything that brings me joy in life before they cause me pain or ruin me.

How fucked up is that?

How fucked up is it that I keep my brother at a distance because one day soon I will have no choice but to hurt him. I don't have another choice but to slowly but painfully distance myself from the other half of me.

Valentino and I have always been different, except for the twin thing of course. When we were children, Valentino loved books and all the other things 'normal' kids enjoyed.

Not me.

I liked seeing papa make grown men cry. I enjoyed how it felt to hold my very first gun, the thrilling feeling of power that ran through my body and made me feel untouchable.

And pain?

I welcome it, like an old friend. Pain makes me feel alive. Pain makes me feel. Period.

I may not be a sociopath like this crazy bitch tries to convince me I am, but I'm not normal and I've never been. I will never be normal or try to fit in with everyone else and I will never play by anyone else's rules.

Rules are meant to be broken and I do love breaking shit.

Especially pretty dolls with fiery red hair.

Just like every time a thought about her appears, I stop that shit real quick.

Can't go there

Not now.

That pussy is jailbait and I like my bitches more experience and not little virginal pageant girls.

I stare at Doctor Whelsh sitting in the chair opposite of me, quietly jotting notes in her journal. I've been coming to this office since I was fourteen years old and there hasn't been a breakthrough. The naive bitch won't give up on me.

There won't be a breakthrough because there's nothing wrong with me. Ok that's bull, there is lots of shit going on in my head that would most likely get me committed.

Fucking Cassius.

Fuck him for putting me through all this unnecessary shit.

And now there's Andrea. Although we didn't learn of her until recently, I feel protective of her.

I touch my neck where her tattoo rests.

She has her eyes.

The same eyes that have haunted me ever since I can remember.

How can I care for someone I have never met? I've known Cassius all of my life and I don't particularly care for him. I don't wish him ill, but I just don't care.

But her...my heart hurts every time I look at her face.

I shake my head and stop the sad thoughts before they consume me. Sometimes I just want to drown in them.

Not today.

I need to be here for Valentino.

For her.

Why did grandfather bring her back after all these years?

He knew she existed, so why now? I don't think for one second that he wants to get the time he lost with her back. The bastard has always known she existed so again...why now?

What's changed?

I want that crown and I want that title, but am I willing to pay the ultimate price?

I know Valentino wants to be the chosen one. He craves chaos, just like I do.

My brother...my fucking brother.

We both knew this day would come. The day where our loyalties will be tested but I never thought it'd hurt this much.

For me to be king, I'll have to sacrifice him.

TRENTADUE

God Or Lucifer

"Well, you can tell Jesus, that the bitch is back."
- Georgina Sparks

Andrea

(6:35 PM) Fallon: Happiest of birthdays queen! Cannot wait to squeeze you!!!!!! Xx

(6:35 PM) Fallon: PS You're free from this hell hole.

(6:36 PM) Fallon: PSS Take me with you :(

FALLON'S TEXTS ARE BITTERSWEET. YES, I'M SO GLAD I AM finally free to go home but the thought of leaving her behind for a couple of months makes my heart ache.

That's what happens when you form bonds with people you'll eventually leave.

I type a quick message back to her and keep scrolling through my phone.

After a long ass day with Lucan, I came back home to take a shower and prepare for the birthday bash Benedetto is throwing me.

I took a break to gather my thoughts since my head has been a dumpster of emotions and revelations lately. To take my mind off everything, I decided to check my messages. I have been avoiding my phone and social media all day since I'm in no mood to answer fake congratulatory messages from strangers and ex-friends and honestly, I'm in no mood to celebrate.

What's there to celebrate anyway?

The first birthday without the woman that gave me life. The first birthday without hearing her god-awful voice singing me happy birthday or making me my "magical" birthday cupcakes. Mom used to go all out for my birthday. She used to say it was the most important day of the year for her.

Fuck, this is so depressing.

I notice I have a missed call from Emilio and a few messages on my social media pages. Most from people I don't know. I've been meaning to return his calls, but I keep forgetting to. He'll bite my ear off once he gets a hold of me.

The ruckus downstairs is giving me a headache. When I entered the house once Lucan dropped me off, I was greeted by some of the maids and bodyguards wishing me a happy birthday.

That was the moment I found out Benedetto planned an over-the-top birthday party for me and invited every member of the three families, students from Holy Trinity, and some business associates of his.

The last thing I want to do today is celebrate and pretend that I'm happy. I'm sick and tired of pretending that it doesn't hurt, that I'm not dying a little bit inside knowing that I'll end up like her soon.

I was headed upstairs with the bags of clothes Lucan got me. My birthday presents, he said.

It was kind of sweet, but I can't let myself be fooled by him.

There's nothing sweet about him.

I do appreciate the distraction. The entire day made me forget that we stanmon opposite sides and want different things. He clearly wants to be the head of the three families and I just want to be free.

Free in New York, doing what I love.

Ok, yes, I like him, but it annoys me to no end.

Having feelings for him makes me vulnerable and he will find a way to take advantage of that. But today felt different. It felt like the start of something new, good, or bad, I do not know but still it felt like something.

I felt it in the way he acted towards me today. His touch felt like a lover's caress and not one of an enemy. He has feelings for me, but I am not naive. He might want me, but he wants to be capo more.

And I know he will do anything to achieve his goal.

There is no future for us.

KNOCK KNOCK.

"It's open!" I scream to the person on the other side of my door.

Roberta appears with a frown on her face.

As usual.

"You're late for your own party.", her icy tone doesn't match the twinkle in her eyes.

"Oh, come on Berta. You won't even wish me a happy birthday? You wound me." I feign hurt and touch my chest in a soothing manner. I must be drunk already with all those shots I took crying on the bathroom floor before I got dressed for the party. Because I see her lips twitching almost forming a smile but of course she won't allow herself to do so.

"Happy Birthday, Miss Nicolasi." She hands me a tiny box with a big red bow. "This was left outside your door", she puts it down on the bed and shuts the door behind her when she leaves.

I look for a card to see who sent it but there isn't one. I'm about to open it when there's another knock on my door.

"Move it, Ms. Nicolasi! The guests are waiting for you!"

"I'm going, I'm going! I get up from my bed, drop the box on the nightstand and walk to the mirror to add the finishing touches on my makeup.

My high ponytail sits perfectly on top of my head. I chose the red dress that Lucan bought me today and added some matching red stilettos.

I feel my neck for my mom's necklace and there's nothing there.

Fuck!

I forgot to ask Lucan for it back. *How could I forget to demand that he give it back? Ugh, I'll do it tonight.*

I forget about the necklace and add my signature blood-red lipstick and once I'm done, I head out the door.

When I reach the stairs, I'm awestruck at how beautiful the mansion looks tonight and how many people came out to celebrate.

The entire place is filled with vanilla scented candles, balloons on every corner and pink decorations.

Again, with the fucking pink.

Damn, the Nicolasi Don went all out for my birthday. I'm

sure he did it for appearances, but whatever.

Benedetto notices me at the top of the stairs first, he signals the band and lame ass birthday music begins to play while I walk down the stairs.

I feel like I did on my *quinceañero*. The Puerto Rican and more extravagant version of a Sweet Sixteen.

I feel everyone's eyes on me. Some look at me with awe, some with curiosity, and others with animosity.

The music stops and grandfather approaches me. "Happy Birthday, *mia cara*." he kisses both of my cheeks. "I hope this is the first of many birthdays we spend together, my dear." he releases my hand and looks around the room.

This feels like when Judas kissed Jesus before selling him out to Pontius Pilate to be crucified. *Wait, is that how the story goes?*

Shit, I really should go to church more often. I'll probably catch fire once I step a foot in God's home.

"Thank you, grandpa." I offer him a fake smile and I kiss his left cheek. "You didn't have to do all this." *Someone, please give me the award for best actress.*

"Nonsense, of course, I did.", he takes my hand and guides me to the middle of the room. "Today we celebrate you *bambina*, enjoy it."

With one last hug, he leaves me standing in the middle of the room while everyone continues talking amongst themselves.

I turn around and find Lucan in a sea of people.

Oh, I will.

Lucan

GOD OR LUCIFER, WHOEVER THE HELL CREATED THIS girl, really worked overtime on her.

Fuck me but she is one hot piece of ass.

From the moment she walked down the stairs, all I could see was her. Everyone stopped what they were doing and focused solely on her.

She looks smoking in that short-as-fuck red dress and that devious smirk painted red.

Yup, the devil definitely had a hand in creating this chick.

A few hours with Andrea have me wanting to say fuck you to my task and keep her for myself.

When I left her for a few moments alone in my house, I took the opportunity to ask Giana to keep Arianna away from Andrea this evening. I need more time before everything explodes in my face.

I'm still staring at her ass when the little vixen catches me staring and a seductive and devious grin forms on her gorgeous face.

Fuck me, this girl has me all fucked in the head.

She's playing with me.

The little devil needs to know that I'm not the one to fuck with unless I am doing the fucking myself.

Hard and dirty fucks are my favorite kind, and I don't appreciate being teased.

Ah shit, now I'm hard just thinking about Andrea and a rough fuck.

She is a walking and talking contradiction and tonight she looks like Lucifer's wife herself. I can't fucking wait to make this *principessa* beg and scream.

Just for me.

I'm about to approach her when a pink haired chick enthusiastically hugs Andrea and snatches her away.

What a cockblock.

Now, I just have to find a way to get her alone.

TRENTATRE

You Are Fucking Mine

"I don't think Jesus would approve of that."
– Blair Waldorf

Andrea

"HAPPY BIRTHDAY BITCH!" FALLON WRAPS HER ARMS around me and almost squeezes the life out of me.

"OMG!" I stare at her hair; it is baby pink now. "You dyed your hair!!" *I didn't notice her before; the alcohol must be clouding my mind.*

She shakes her head from side to side and smirks. "I needed a change. Do you like it?" She runs her fingers through the luscious baby-pink strands.

"Hell yes, I do! You look like a sexy nymph." She really does. Tonight, there's nothing nerdy about Fallon's appearance. She has a black low-cut dress making her impressive rack look hot as hell and she added some black lipstick.

She looks like a woman on a mission.

A mission to make a guy regret ever letting her go.

That's my girl.

She hasn't told me the story with Valentino, but I'll be here when she decides to open up.

Fallon takes my hand and leads me to the middle of the room where a couple of the guests are dancing. The proper thing to do is to mingle with the guests and thank them for coming but I honestly don't give a fuck about appearances.

Not tonight.

"You should know everyone from Holy T is here," she shouts over the loud music. "Even the botched blondes.", she rolls her eyes and reaches for two cups of punch. Fallon is awfully chatty and happy tonight.

I bring one cup to my nose and like I suspected, there's alcohol in it and my girl is hammered.

This will be an interesting night.

THE NIGHT IS FLYING BY SO FAST AND I HAVEN'T SEEN Lucan all night. Either he's with one of the guys or some girl has latched on to him.

I love Fallon and I'm thankful she's here, but I need a break. I need to be alone for a couple of minutes. So, I left her with Lucan's sisters and excused myself.

I leave the party and head to the pool house. It's peaceful here and I need some time to myself. It's easy to forget when there are people around you but when you're alone...yeah loneliness is an ugly bitch and it won't let me forget that even in a crowded room, I'm still so alone.

"Looking for me, *principessa*?", my own personal and sexy as hell nightmare whispers in my ear.

"Cocky much, Volpe?", his raspy laugh causes goosebumps to breakout all over my skin. Nothing has ever sounded so hot before.

"Oh, baby girl, wouldn't you like to know?" So damn arrogant, this one. I must admit that his confidence works for him. I won't let him know he affects me. I rather stick my eye out.

"I'm not one of your many conquests, Lucan. Don't treat me as one." I stare as his eyes and a weird look crossed over his face, but I don't have to go decipher it.

In one swift movement, he grabs my neck from behind and turns my face so he can have easy access to my mouth. His hold on my neck is too much and I'm hot all over.

"Listen to me and listen carefully because I'm not one to repeat myself, princess.", his hold on my neck loosens and I can breathe again. "I decided I'm keeping you, and there's no one in this fucked up world that will keep me from you. I'm too far-gone baby, there's no saving me.", he whispers before sucking my bottom lip and gently nibbling on it.

Who knew pain could feel so good?

Sweet torture.

"Come on, I'm hungry.", he grabs my hand and pulls me with him.

Huh?

"There is cake inside if you want," I tell him lamely.

I'm dripping wet and he's hungry, seriously?

I don't even know why I'm considering jumping his fun pole but I am. I'm blaming it on the alcohol. Yes, that's the only reason I would ever jump in bed with this infuriating jerk.

Ok, I'm not wasted, I know what I'm doing. I can't really blame it on the alcohol.

"I'm hungry but not for food." He grabs my hand, leads us inside the pool house and once we're in, he locks the door and faces me with a look of pure unadulterated hunger on his face. "I'm dying for a taste of you, *principessa*."

He kisses me once more, but this time sweet and slow before lifting me up and carrying me to the bed.

I've had sex before but somehow Lucan is making me feel like I did on my first time.

I can just imagine all the dirty things he wants to do to my body. Hell, I get wet just thinking about all the dirty things I want to do to his body.

He slowly starts to unzip his pants and takes his sweet time doing it.

He's torturing me when all I want to do is see all of him. Every single glorious part of him.

I can't control the moan that escapes me when his thick and long length is set free.

I'm still staring at his hard cock, when he grabs me by the neck and pulls me towards him. I can feel his dick on my stomach, and I swear I could come just from the feel of him on my skin.

"Do you like what you're seeing, *principessa*?", he's biting his lip and trying to hide his smile.

"I want your cock in my mouth." I bite my lip while I look into his eyes.

The groan that leaves his mouth makes me rub my legs together to relieve the ache.

He's so annoyingly hot.

Lucan not so gently pushes me back down onto the bed. "You can choke on it another time baby. Right now, I want your juices all over my face.", he grabs me by the knees and maneuvers me until I'm on top of him. "Fucking ride my face."

I feel his hot breath near my center before he parts my pussy lips with his tongue.

"Ahh, that feels so good baby. Don't stop." The things this man can do with his tongue should be illegal. He starts to slowly swipe his tongue up and down and I'm about to lose it.

"Don't fucking come. Not until I'm deep inside you."

My head falls back, and my knees start to shake but before I can reach sweet oblivion, he stops.

"You are evil." I groan and fall back on the bed, still high from the near orgasm.

"Shut the fuck up and come here." I feel Lucan lift my leg and wrap it around his waist. He starts rubbing his dick up and down my wet slit making my eyes roll to the back of my head.

"Are you a virgin baby?", he rasps.

"Sorry to disappoint you handsome, but no."

He takes my bottom lip between his teeth. "Good," he whispers before he thrust inside me without warning.

I gasp from the sudden intrusion. My screams of pleasure are muffled by his hand covering my mouth all the while he starts to slam into me relentlessly.

I like this side of him. When he loses control and lets his wild side roam free.

I feel him everywhere as he pushes into me repeatedly and has me curling my toes and biting my lip until I taste blood.

He notices it and slows his pace before sucking my bloody lip and moaning like he never tasted anything as good as me before.

There's no noise in the room. Just the sound of our slick, wet skin slapping together so loudly that even the party going on outside couldn't drown the sound.

I'm so lost in him that the world outside is lost to me.

He does something that surprises me though. He grabs my

face in the gentlest of ways and stares into my eyes. "Say you're mine.", he grounds out.

"You first." I tease him. He didn't stand me a couple of hours ago and now wants to claim me? The heat of the moment is making him say these things.

"Yes, fucking yours.", he hisses while trying to fuck the words out of me.

"Come now, baby," he grits through clenched teeth and moves one of his hands down until he finds my clit. He tortures me until I give in and give him what he wants.

I cry out once he hits that spot that makes my eyes roll back and has me screaming that I'm his.

"There's no going back, *principessa*.", his thrusts are wilder and more animalistic now.

"You are fucking mine."

Shit, those final words shake me to my core.

TRENTAQUATTRO

Just Like Her Mother

"Why are you so obsessed with me?"
- Regina George

Andrea

I JUST GOT FUCKED WITHIN AN INCH OF MY LIFE.

Seriously, I can't seem to find my breath and my legs are numb.

Lucan is still on top of me and I can feel the erratic beating of his heart. He's quiet and lost in thought while playing with a tendril of my hair. His mouth finds mine, and I sense his desperation.

"I'm so sorry, *principessa*," he says between kisses. "Let's go away, just the two of us, somewhere we can be alone without distractions", he sounds desperate, almost pleading with me.

I laugh at the thought. Yeah, like we could just drop everything, and no one will question us.

"Just yesterday you disliked me, now what? My pussy is so good that you're willing to drop everything and leave?"

He lifts his head from my chest and stares at me with this solemn look that makes me feel like I just made the worst mistake of my life.

"What's going on Lucan?" I have this dreadful feeling now that I can't shake.

"Look Andrea, there's something I need to tell you but please remember how you felt in my arms."

"What did you do?" I push him off the bed and grab my panties off the floor before hurrying to slip them back on. My hands are shaking now. What the hell is wrong with me?

"You should know that I didn't—", he's interrupted by a loud knock on the pool house door.

"Drea, you in there?", I hear Fallon in the distance calling out for me.

She shouts louder now. "They're ready to sing happy birthday and your grandfather is looking for you!"

Shit.

"I'll be right there." I fix my hair in the mirror as fast as I can, trying to hide the fact that I just got fucked within an inch of my life.

I leave Lucan with his regrets and his secrets.

I'm so fucking stupid.

"Andrea, fucking wait!", he reaches for my hand but I'm faster and I slip out of the room before he can spew more bullshit.

THE GUESTS JUST FINISHED SINGING ME HAPPY BIRTHDAY and now everyone is eating cake while talking amongst themselves.

I'm still confused about what went down with Lucan. He seemed so sincere when he declared he was mine and I was his.

Now he's nowhere to be found and my annoying thoughts are clouding my judgement.

"Look, isn't that you Andrea?", Cassia shouts from the living room.

I hear whispers in the background, but I can't make out anything they're saying.

Oh...no...

This can't be happening.

"This is just in, the true cause of death of the late Valeria Turner, CEO of Valentina Co. and once one of the highest-paid supermodels in the world, was just revealed." The newsman is about to reveal my greatest fear to the world.

How did this happen?

The room is eerily quiet. Everyone is waiting for that piece of gossip that gives them leverage against me.

"Sources close to Andrea Turner, the eighteen-year-old daughter of Valeria say that the late supermodel turned fashion mogul suffered from a fatal infection due to dementia." — This is not real. I tried so hard to hide it. — "In her last days on earth, she didn't remember her daughter, not even her own name."

My ears are ringing, my vision is blurry and all I can hear over and over again is the man on the TV — "she didn't remember her daughter." —, there is a gasp behind me, and I feel a gentle hand on my shoulder.

Fallon joined me in the middle of the room. I'm so numb I don't even feel her gentle touch.

I shake her hands off and turn around to face the room.

They're all here.

They know my secret now.

Benedetto has a knowing look. Valentino and Lorenzo share the same look of grief, and Cassius...he drops a glass of wine to the floor and the look of pain behind his stare is one that I will always remember.

The sound of a door being opened and footsteps nearing me makes me look away from the room and look straight at the one person that had enough motives to do this.

Lucan told the media about my mother, but how did he find out?

Did Emilio...? No, he wouldn't have. He loved mom dearly. I refuse to believe he sold us out.

It must've been Lucan.

I was too busy getting fucked by him while my entire world was crumbling.

How could I be so naive?

Not only does the world know about my mom, but now they'll have everything they need to prove I'm not competent to run my mother's company.

What did I do...?

Lucan

FUCK.

I was an idiot for believing the gossip site Arianna sold the news to, wouldn't run the piece and stop everyone from finding out what truly happened to Andrea's mom. I fucking tried to stop this from happening, but it was too late. Arianna sold the news and now everything is ruined.

Without us even really starting, I ended us.

"Who told you?" I will never forget the look of complete devastation and betrayal on Andrea's beautiful eyes.

"*Principessa*, listen to me please. I tried to stop them from releasing the news, but I was too late." I try to reason but it's useless, I fucked up. "Baby, I..."

"Who fucking told you!?", she shouts sounding like a wounded animal.

I feel like the biggest piece of shit alive and I wish I could go back in time and stop this shit show from happening.

"Baby, I'm so sorry." I try reaching for her, but she steps back as if my touch hurts her.

Maybe it does.

Everything I touch I ruin.

"You're sorry for telling the world about my mother's last days? For tainting her image?", she lowers her voice so only I can hear. "Or are you sorry for fucking me after you conspired against me?" There's so much hurt and venom in her voice.

I won't be able to fix this.

"You need to understand..."

Slap!

She slapped me, she fucking slapped me.

"Listen to me, Lucan." The look in her eyes scares me more than whatever is about to come out of her mouth. — "We? Whatever this was. It ends here." — With that said, she turns her back on me —on us—and leaves.

She is fucking delusional if she thinks it'll be that easy to get away from me. "You are mine!" I shout at her retreating back. "You said the fucking words *principessa* and there is no going back, I'll get you back no matter the price. On that you have my word."

Why the fuck did I think that we could ever be more than rivals? I just proved that everything I touch...I fucking ruin.

But she's wrong.

This thing between us?

It isn't over. It'll never end.

I didn't lie to her when I said I was hers and that she was goddamn mine. No one will keep us apart.

Not even her.

I feel a slender, feminine arm around me. Arianna. "You did it, Luc. You got rid of her for good. There's no way she'll be head of any family now. If she's anything like her mother, she'll soon forget."

An evil grin takes over Arianna's face, one I've never witnessed on her before. She was always cold and selfish but never cruel.

I turn around and face the mess I have caused. Everyone is still whispering about Andrea and in the background the anchor lady is reporting the news, talking about what this will mean to the future of Andrea's company.

I keep staring at the tv, but I zone everyone out, focusing on Arianna's words.

What she said about Andrea, keeps playing in my head on a never-ending loop.

"You got rid of her for good."

"If she's anything like her mother she'll soon forget."

"She'll soon forget."

"Forget..."

Fuck!

TRENTACINQUE

My Only Ally

"Listen, Sandy. Men are rats."
- Frenchy

Andrea

KNOCK KNOCK.

"Andrea, please let me in!" I feel bad for ignoring Fallon, but I just want to be alone. Like I should've stayed all along and avoided the disappointment and betrayal.

I brought this upon myself.

I really did.

I didn't lie to Lucan when I told him I've had sex before, but I've never told anyone that I was theirs.

For one night I gave him everything I had to give.

I've never felt this used before and I should have expected this to happen, but for once I thought that I wouldn't be burned by love.

Why does everyone leave me?

After excusing myself from the party, I came up to my room and ripped the dress Lucan gifted me to pieces. I need to find a way to make him regret this humiliation and soon.

I'm so ashamed.

I let myself be played but this won't break me.

I had one mission and that was to find out what happened to my father and now I know. I can get the fuck out of this town now but there's no way the family will let one of their own live a peaceful life without a price being paid. The only way for me to get back to New York and focus on my mom's dream is to take down the three families or rule them. Now that they found out about my mother's disease and that I might possibly carry the gene, there's no way they'll consider me fit to lead them.

If I can't lead the families, then I guess their empire will have to crumble and burn until there's nothing left but their shame and broken egos.

Benedetto tried to talk to me, but I don't want to see him either. He is guilty of something and his loyalty is not to me.

There's a loud noise outside my door and someone pushes the door open. "I said I want to be alone."

"You know Andrea, you shouldn't waste your tears on people that do not deserve them. Especially that Volpe scum.", he says with obvious disdain.

I never expected him to visit me tonight.

How dare he approach me after what he's done to my family?

"*Mio sole*, penso che dovresti ascoltarmi. Il tempo sta finendo." Cassius says in Italian but I have a hard time understanding him.

"My sunshine, I think you should hear me out." I'm seconds away from throwing him out but the term of endearment catches me off guard and renders me speechless.

"What...What did you just call me?" How does he know? The only person that called me sunshine is dead.

He looks at me with so much love and pain mixed together. And then he tells me the one thing I never saw coming.

"My sunshine.", he sits in the bed facing me before he continues. "Andrea, you are my child, and your mother was my life."

What...the...fuck...

This must be some sort of joke.

"Why would I believe anything that comes out of the mouth of a drunk?"— I want to hurt him like he's hurting me by making up lies. He visibly flinches and I feel guilty, but why should I believe him?

"That's fair," he reaches for something on my nightstand. The gift Berta left earlier for me. "Maybe, you'll believe Valeria, huh?" He offers it to me, and I don't hesitate before ripping the paper off and opening the small box.

Inside, there's a necklace fit for a small child identical to the one that Lucan stole from me, my mom' necklace. This one has a locket and I know what's inside will change everything.

My hands are shaking as Cassius opens the locket for me to see.

Inside, there's a picture of a much younger him and...my mom.

They look so happy and so in love with a chubby baby girl between them.

I can't hold back the tears that threatened to spill, because although I made my mom smile, it was never like that.

Like she discovered the meaning of life and she didn't need anything else. Just Cassius and me.

"How is this possible?" I look up at him and there's so much love in his gaze that I find it almost impossible to breathe.

"I'll tell you everything, *mia vita*." he pulls a small envelope out of his suit jacket and hands it to me. "But first your mother has something to say to you."

I don't let a second longer pass before I'm ripping the letter off his hands and opening it.

A letter from my only ally.

My mom.

TRENTASEI

My Strong Girl

"But to cry in front of you, that's the worst thing I could do."
- Rizzo

My dearest sunshine,

I am sorry.

You will never know how sorry I am that I couldn't fight for you, for us. I am sorry that if you are reading this that I am no longer with you. I am sorry that I might forget you but know this, mi amor: Even when my mind forgets, my heart will always remember you. I am sorry for a lot of things...

I am not sorry that I lied to you, it kept you safe. It kept that beautiful little heart that gave my life so much meaning, beating.

But I guess now I should tell you what I didn't have the chance to do in life. It was not the right time yet.

It is now.

You see my love: I fell in love with a man that couldn't keep me even when all he wanted to do was that. Your father comes from a very powerful family, a family *that did not accept us, me. Before your father met me, he was promised to another woman, the daughter of the Volpe capo. The arrangement was done so the two families could become one, your father as the firstborn son was destined to be capo but he refused to do so, and as you can imagine that did not go well with your grandfather. He wouldn't allow it. Cassius did not care and ran away with me. We were blissfully happy until they found us.*

Benedetto disowned your father, and your uncle Demetrio was set to take his place until you happened. From the purest of love, you were born. You were everything we always wanted Andrea, what we always dreamed of.

You and them.

Our story is too complicated to explain over a letter. Your father will answer everything I can't. You must not trust anyone my love, just your father.

He saved us once, let him do it again.

I never wanted this life for you. I never wanted to leave you to deal with all of this on your own.

Now, I know you are wondering why I lied about your father being Demetrio Nicolasi. I had no choice. He was a bad man Andrea, and not only is he the worst of them all, but he is also your grandfather's pride and joy. He always wanted what your father had... and he wanted me. We had no choice but to agree to his demands because we couldn't risk your life.

Now I need you to remember everything I taught
you, — be ruthless, be brave, and most importantly,
be you.

There's no one quite like you.

I loved you with everything that was left of my heart.
I loved you then and I will love you forever...

I am sorry.

Forever yours,

Mom.

TRENTASETTE

VAL

"I want more."
– Sharpay Evans

Andrea

THE TEARS THAT I'VE BEEN HOLDING BACK FALL ONTO MY cheeks and I'm too tired to hold them back.

I let Cassius see me break.

My father.

Looking back now at our brief interactions, he was always gentle and never rude.

"I don't understand. I thought my father was Demetrio," I look at Cassius, really look at him, for the first time since I met him. He has the same chin dimple as me, the same as...

Shit.

"The twins, they're my half-siblings?"

"They're your blood brothers Andrea. I never had anyone after your mother."

Looking at him after this revelation, something catches my eyes, a gold chain on his neck. I reach for it and it has the same initials as the one mom left me.

A thought forms in my head, but I need answers.

Still holding the chain, I ask: "v-a-l is not short for Valeria is it?" I stare into my father's eyes, the same man that only just minutes ago I thought ruined my family. "It's the initials of our names.", I whisper.

Valentino

Andrea

Lorenzo

"Yes, *mia figlia*, our three greatest loves." The looks in his eyes warms me. There's so much hurt and love in his eyes.

Love for me?

"But how?" There are no photos of mom and a second pregnancy! I can't believe this, I'm so confused, and nothing makes sense anymore.

Was my entire life a lie?

"Andrea, we are running out of time", Cassius reaches under my bed and hands me a bag. Wait, was that there this entire time?

"We need to go. I promise I'll tell you everything but for now, you need to trust me. Trust your mother.", he gets up from the bed and offers me his hand. "We can't stay under the same roof as your grandfather, he can't be trusted anymore."

"If I go with you, will you tell me everything?" I ask him. "No more fucking lies."

"Yes, *mia cara*. I'll tell you everything there is to know," he opens the door for me and leads me outside the mansion. It's almost morning, so everyone is still sleeping.

Outside, there's a black escalade ready for us. The door is opened by none other than Lorenzo himself. "Move it, big sis, they're waiting for us."

Where is Valentino? Why isn't he here? I wonder.

I stare at Cassius' amused face, "Where are we going?" I ask confused by this all.

"Home," he ushers me inside the car and before he closes the door he says:

"New York."

I get in the car with my newfound brother and father and leave this fucking city behind.

I have no idea what is waiting for me back in New York but because of Lucan exposing the true nature of my mother's demise, I am sure nothing, but trouble is waiting for me back in my world.

I still do not know who to trust. My mother wouldn't lie to me, not about something this big. I have to trust Cassius.

I have no choice.

My mother's secret was exposed to the world and now her legacy is being threaten. Her empire just went up in flames all because I let myself be fooled by Lucan. He threaten what matters most to me and he will pay.

Maybe not tomorrow but someday.

I will make him pay.

Everyone that was involved.

One day I will watch his world burn down in flames while sitting back in my throne.

The king will fall and so will the Holy Trinity of Detroit.

Even if it kills me.

It just might.

TRENTOTTO

Only Truths

"Some people are worth melting for."
- Olaf

Cassius

WE ARE TWO HOURS AWAY FROM REACHING OUR destination and that means my girl is safe. Benedetto can touch her here. None of the families can attack her outside of Holy territory.

I knew my father hated me; I've always known but his hatred won't touch my children.

I won't allow it.

I believed Benedetto when he gave me his word that as long as I stayed anyway from both of them, they were safe from any harm.

My only worry right this instant is Valentino. He chose to stay with his grandfather back in Detroit. My son chose the family over his family. But why? My boy has always been outspoken and has let me know more than a couple hundred times how much he despises the made life.

So why did he choose to stay? I cannot keep him safe from here, but I am relieved to know that he will have Rian watching his back. The Nicolasi soldier swore his loyalty to me and me only. He despises Benedetto almost as much as I do.

Almost.

Andrea's voice in the background gives me no choice but to snap out of it and I give her my full attention instead of worrying about my youngest son.

"Come again *mia figlia*?" My daughter. After years of watching her from afar, now I have her here with me where she was always meant to be. I always knew this day would come but not so soon. She was supposed to know the truth after she turned twenty-one.

Not now.

This was all his doing.

Benedetto didn't play fair and now my children are in danger from their own family just because of my past mistakes. They shouldn't have to carry my sins on their backs.

It was not supposed to be this way.

"Why did you leave us?" Andrea whispers so softly that I almost miss it. As if she's afraid of what my answer will be.

How do I explain to my girl that I destroyed what mattered most to my father? And now after all this time, he found a way to make me pay.

He would hurt his grandchildren just to see me bleed.

It wasn't enough that he split my family up for years and now he is using my children to get back at me.

All of this because I fell in love and he punished me for it.

They both did.

"I am the eldest son, and it was my duty to take over the city once your grandfather stepped down, but I fell in love instead and I refused." I still remember that day like it was yesterday. The disappointment in my father's face and Demetrio's reaction once

I told them I had no plans to be capo. "I didn't want this life for you and your mother." I take a deep breath before continuing. This is the hardest part. "The only way to keep you safe from my world was to leave both of you safe in New York, but your mother and I were selfish and couldn't stay away. We thought we had everyone fooled and then the year you turned one, the twins were born. We were so happy, but our happiness didn't last long." I stare into my daughter's eyes and let her see the honesty in mine.

"Tell me everything." She's too calm for someone that's been betrayed and exposed all in one day.

So, I give my daughter my truths.

Only truths.

"I know you were there the night I was arguing with your grandfather. You heard me when I said that I killed my brother." I need her to believe me.

"Yes, I killed my brother, the apple of Benedetto's eye and I do not regret it. Not for one second. He threatened my life, my children and my love." I make sure I'm loud enough that Lorenzo is able to hear me as well. I planned to tell them all together, but Valentino gave me no choice.

"I would kill the son of a bitch again if I had the opportunity. Demetrio's jealousy was always greater than his love for me."

His greed and envy were both of our downfall.

The day he fell from grace, he dragged me to hell with him.

Valeria was mine, but my twin brother always wanted everything I had so he did everything he could to keep us apart.

I saw her first.

I loved her first.

Demetrio got away with separating my family because of a whim but his last threat was the last straw.

No one fucks with my kids' lives and gets to live another day.

I hope my brother is burning in hell.

Now, Benedetto, he gave me his word that Andrea would stay safe in her world, but I should've known his word means shit.

I'll take care of my father in due time. Now, I need to focus on how to help my girl conquer this new challenge.

They will try to take her mother's legacy away based on Valeria's cause of death.

Fatal infection.

Dementia.

Fuck that heartless bitch that took so much from my love.

She had no memory of me.

On her deathbed she didn't remember our love.

My Andrea won't suffer the same fate.

She won't.

The End.
For now.

ACKNOWLEDGMENTS

I'm so thankful for everyone in this community that supports all of my crazy ideas. From my IG accounts to my YouTube Channel and now this new adventure. From the first moment I announced I had a story that I wanted to share with you, but I was scared to do so since I am not a writer and well, I've never done this before, you decided to give me a chance and push me to conquer my fear and publish this book. I love reading and I love that feeling of peace I get every time I read a story and it helps me escape to another world for just a couple of hours or maybe even days.

Thank you to my queen, who, during this new and exciting adventure supported me every step of the way even when she felt I was doing too much or felt anxious for me. I am forever grateful to God for choosing me as your daughter. I love you beyond words can express mom, you make me want to do better and want better for myself.

Thank you, Thalia, for helping me through this release, from marketing, to emotional support and everything in between. I couldn't have done this without you. You helped me so much and I am forever grateful to you. Not only are you a wonderful friend but you are a phenomenal writer.

To the best beta, proofreader, and blogger/friend I was lucky enough to meet in this community, Elsa. You decided to help me through all this crazy process, from proof reading, to plotting, to edits and making sure the book was ready to be published. I am also forever grateful for you. I also couldn't have done this without you. The moment you told me the book was not crap, LOL, I felt immensely happy and I decided to really go through with this. Thank you!

Gisele, you are the most genuine and the most creative person I've met on here and your account is the absolute best, but you already know this. Thank you for helping me and doing the most beautiful edits that helped so much with promo. You saved my promo and my Instagram account. Love you!!

Juddeh, thank you so much for believing in my words when I didn't. For reading all the versions of this story, never complaining, and rooting for me instead. Thank you for being an inspiration and such an amazing friend.

To my beta friends, Hass, Katie and Jazzy – you guys are wonderful and offered me the best feedback. Thank you for taking a chance on me. I am so grateful to have you on my team.

My wonderful ARC team/Girl squad, I am forever grateful for everything you do for me. You make posts and beautiful edits, and it makes my heart so happy.

Alexis, the best PA. Thank you for everything you do and for always being on top of everything. You are such a wonderful friend and I'm so happy you're in my corner.

And to the readers and bloggers, thank you for giving me a chance. You may like the book or maybe you won't but that's okay because you took a chance on me and on this weird world of mafia and strong girls who fall for psychotic boys. Thank you for being so supportive and kind. You deserve so much for all the work you do for authors and for this community. Forever thankful for you.

Much love, Always,

Adriana.

About the Author

Adriana Brinne is a new author, who fell in love with reading from a very young age, but never felt brave enough to share her words with the world. She was born and raised in a tropical island surrounded by only beauty and water called Puerto Rico. She is a full time IT engineer, and, on her downtime, you can find her reading new adult romances by her favorite authors, reviewing books and watching The Big Bang Theory.

She has a love for all things dark in romance and almost every trope created except cheating and the death trope. She hates them and you won't catch her writing or reading about it. The Holy Trinity characters are screaming to have their stories told and she plans to do just that. From her, you can expect all the feels, strong girls and asshole heroes that worship the ground they walk on.

Printed in Germany
by Amazon Distribution
GmbH, Leipzig

23279935R00136